Best Short Stories

Guy de Maupassant

THE NECKLACE

The girl was one of those pretty and charming young creatures who sometimes are born, as if by a slip of fate, into a family of clerks. She had no dowry, no expectations, no way of being known, understood, loved, married by any rich and distinguished man; so she let herself be married to a little clerk of the Ministry of Public Instruction.

She dressed plainly because she could not dress well, but she was unhappy as if she had really fallen from a higher station; since with women there is neither caste nor rank, for beauty, grace and charm take the place of family and birth. Natural ingenuity, instinct for what is elegant, a supple mind are their sole hierarchy, and often make of women of the people the equals of the very greatest ladies.

Mathilde suffered ceaselessly, feeling herself born to enjoy all delicacies and all luxuries. She was distressed at the poverty of her dwelling, at the bareness of the walls, at the shabby chairs, the ugliness of the curtains. All those things, of which another woman of her rank would never even have been conscious, tortured her and made her angry. The sight of the little Breton peasant who did her humble housework aroused in her despairing regrets and bewildering dreams. She thought of silent antechambers hung with Oriental tapestry, illumined by tall bronze candelabra, and of two great footmen in knee breeches who sleep in the big armchairs, made drowsy by the oppressive heat of the stove. She thought of long reception halls hung with ancient silk, of the dainty cabinets containing priceless curiosities and of the little coquettish perfumed reception rooms made for chatting at five o'clock with intimate friends, with men famous and sought after, whom all women envy and whose attention they all desire.

When she sat down to dinner, before the round table covered with a tablecloth in use three days, opposite her husband, who uncovered the soup tureen and declared with a delighted air, "Ah, the good soup! I don't know anything better than that," she thought of dainty dinners, of shining silverware, of tapestry that peopled the walls with ancient personages and with strange birds flying in the midst of a fairy forest; and she thought of delicious dishes served on marvellous plates and of the whispered gallantries to which you listen with a sphinxlike smile while you are eating the pink meat of a trout or the wings of a quail.

She had no gowns, no jewels, nothing. And she loved nothing but that. She felt made for that. She would have liked so much to please, to be envied, to be charming, to be sought after.

She had a friend, a former schoolmate at the convent, who was rich, and whom she did not like to go to see any more because she felt so sad when she came home.

But one evening her husband reached home with a triumphant air and holding a large envelope in his hand.

"There," said he, "there is something for you."

She tore the paper quickly and drew out a printed card which bore these words:

The Minister of Public Instruction and Madame Georges Ramponneau request the honor of M. and Madame Loisel's company at the palace of the Ministry on Monday evening, January 18th.

Instead of being delighted, as her husband had hoped, she threw the invitation on the table crossly, muttering:

"What do you wish me to do with that?"

"Why, my dear, I thought you would be glad. You never go out, and this is such a fine opportunity. I had great trouble to get it. Every one wants to go; it is very select, and they are not giving many invitations to clerks. The whole official world will be there."

She looked at him with an irritated glance and said impatiently:

"And what do you wish me to put on my back?"

He had not thought of that. He stammered:

5

"Why, the gown you go to the theatre in. It looks very well to me."

He stopped, distracted, seeing that his wife was weeping. Two great tears ran slowly from the corners of her eyes toward the corners of her mouth.

"What's the matter? What's the matter?" he answered.

By a violent effort she conquered her grief and replied in a calm voice, while she wiped her wet cheeks:

"Nothing. Only I have no gown, and, therefore, I can't go to this ball. Give your card to some colleague whose wife is better equipped than I am."

He was in despair. He resumed:

"Come, let us see, Mathilde. How much would it cost, a suitable gown, which you could use on other occasions--something very simple?"

She reflected several seconds, making her calculations and wondering also what sum she could ask without drawing on herself an immediate refusal and a frightened exclamation from the economical clerk.

Finally she replied hesitating:

"I don't know exactly, but I think I could manage it with four hundred francs."

He grew a little pale, because he was laying aside just that amount to buy a gun and treat himself to a little shooting next summer on the plain of Nanterre, with several friends who went to shoot larks there of a Sunday.

But he said:

"Very well. I will give you four hundred francs. And try to have a pretty gown."

The day of the ball drew near and Madame Loisel seemed sad, uneasy, anxious. Her frock was ready, however. Her husband said to her one evening:

"What is the matter? Come, you have seemed very queer these last three days."

And she answered:

"It annoys me not to have a single piece of jewelry, not a single ornament, nothing to put on. I shall look poverty-stricken. I would almost rather not go at all."

"You might wear natural flowers," said her husband. "They're very stylish at this time of year. For ten francs you can get two or three magnificent roses."

She was not convinced.

"No; there's nothing more humiliating than to look poor among other women who are rich."

"How stupid you are!" her husband cried. "Go look up your friend, Madame Forestier, and ask her to lend you some jewels. You're intimate enough with her to do that."

She uttered a cry of joy:

"True! I never thought of it."

The next day she went to her friend and told her of her distress.

Madame Forestier went to a wardrobe with a mirror, took out a large jewel box, brought it back, opened it and said to Madame Loisel:

"Choose, my dear."

She saw first some bracelets, then a pearl necklace, then a Venetian gold cross set with precious stones, of admirable workmanship. She tried on the ornaments before the mirror, hesitated and could not make up her mind to part with them, to give them back. She kept asking:

"Haven't you any more?"

"Why, yes. Look further; I don't know what you like."

Suddenly she discovered, in a black satin box, a superb diamond necklace, and her heart throbbed with an immoderate desire. Her hands trembled as she took it. She fastened it round her throat, outside her high-necked waist, and was lost in ecstasy at her reflection in the mirror.

Then she asked, hesitating, filled with anxious doubt:

"Will you lend me this, only this?"

"Why, yes, certainly."

She threw her arms round her friend's neck, kissed her passionately, then fled with her treasure.

The night of the ball arrived. Madame Loisel was a great success. She was prettier than any other woman present, elegant, graceful, smiling and wild with joy. All the men looked at her, asked her name, sought to be introduced. All the attaches of the Cabinet wished to waltz with her. She was remarked by the minister himself.

She danced with rapture, with passion, intoxicated by pleasure, forgetting all in the triumph of her beauty, in the glory of her success, in a sort of cloud of happiness comprised of all this homage, admiration, these awakened desires and of that sense of triumph which is so sweet to woman's heart.

She left the ball about four o'clock in the morning. Her husband had been sleeping since midnight in a little deserted anteroom with three other gentlemen whose wives were enjoying the ball.

He threw over her shoulders the wraps he had brought, the modest wraps of common life, the poverty of which contrasted with the elegance of the ball dress. She felt this and wished to escape so as not to be remarked by the other women, who were enveloping themselves in costly furs.

Loisel held her back, saying: "Wait a bit. You will catch cold outside. I will call a cab."

But she did not listen to him and rapidly descended the stairs. When they reached the street they could not find a carriage and began to look for one, shouting after the cabmen passing at a distance.

They went toward the Seine in despair, shivering with cold. At last they found on the quay one of those ancient night cabs which, as though they were ashamed to show their shabbiness during the day, are never seen round Paris until after dark.

It took them to their dwelling in the Rue des Martyrs, and sadly they mounted the stairs to their flat. All was ended for her. As to him, he reflected that he must be at the ministry at ten o'clock that morning.

She removed her wraps before the glass so as to see herself once more in all her glory. But suddenly she uttered a cry. She no longer had the necklace around her neck!

"What is the matter with you?" demanded her husband, already half undressed.

She turned distractedly toward him.

"I have--I have--I've lost Madame Forestier's necklace," she cried.

He stood up, bewildered.

"What!--how? Impossible!"

They looked among the folds of her skirt, of her cloak, in her pockets, everywhere, but did not find it.

"You're sure you had it on when you left the ball?" he asked.

"Yes, I felt it in the vestibule of the minister's house."

"But if you had lost it in the street we should have heard it fall. It must be in the cab."

"Yes, probably. Did you take his number?"

"No. And you--didn't you notice it?"

"No."

They looked, thunderstruck, at each other. At last Loisel put on his clothes.

"I shall go back on foot," said he, "over the whole route, to see whether I can find it."

He went out. She sat waiting on a chair in her ball dress, without strength to go to bed, overwhelmed, without any fire, without a thought.

Her husband returned about seven o'clock. He had found nothing.

He went to police headquarters, to the newspaper offices to offer a reward; he went to the cab companies--everywhere, in fact, whither he was urged by the least spark of hope.

She waited all day, in the same condition of mad fear before this terrible calamity.

Loisel returned at night with a hollow, pale face. He had discovered nothing.

"You must write to your friend," said he, "that you have broken the clasp of her necklace and that you are having it mended. That will give us time to turn round."

She wrote at his dictation.

At the end of a week they had lost all hope. Loisel, who had aged five years, declared:

"We must consider how to replace that ornament."

The next day they took the box that had contained it and went to the jeweler whose name was found within. He consulted his books.

"It was not I, madame, who sold that necklace; I must simply have furnished the case."

Then they went from jeweler to jeweler, searching for a necklace like the other, trying to recall it, both sick with chagrin and grief.

They found, in a shop at the Palais Royal, a string of diamonds that seemed to them exactly like the one they had lost. It was worth forty thousand francs. They could have it for thirty-six.

So they begged the jeweler not to sell it for three days yet. And they made a bargain that he should buy it back for thirty-four thousand francs, in case they should find the lost necklace before the end of February.

Loisel possessed eighteen thousand francs which his father had left him. He would borrow the rest.

He did borrow, asking a thousand francs of one, five hundred of another, five louis here, three louis there. He gave notes, took up ruinous obligations, dealt with usurers and all the race of lenders. He compromised all the rest of his life, risked signing a note without even knowing whether he could meet it; and, frightened by the trouble yet to come, by the black misery that was about to fall upon him, by the prospect of all the physical privations and moral tortures that he was to suffer, he went to get the new necklace, laying upon the jeweler's counter thirty-six thousand francs.

When Madame Loisel took back the necklace Madame Forestier said to her with a chilly manner:

"You should have returned it sooner; I might have needed it."

She did not open the case, as her friend had so much feared. If she had detected the substitution, what would she have thought, what would she have said? Would she not have taken Madame Loisel for a thief?

Thereafter Madame Loisel knew the horrible existence of the needy. She bore her part, however, with sudden heroism. That dreadful debt must be paid. She would pay it. They dismissed their servant; they changed their lodgings; they rented a garret under the roof.

She came to know what heavy housework meant and the odious cares of the kitchen. She washed the dishes, using her dainty fingers and rosy nails on greasy pots and pans. She washed the soiled linen, the shirts and the dishcloths, which she dried upon a line; she carried the slops down to the street every morning and carried up the water, stopping for breath at every landing. And dressed like a woman of the people, she went to the fruiterer, the grocer, the butcher, a basket on her arm, bargaining, meeting with impertinence, defending her miserable money, sou by sou.

Every month they had to meet some notes, renew others, obtain more time.

Her husband worked evenings, making up a tradesman's accounts, and late at night he often copied manuscript for five sous a page.

This life lasted ten years.

At the end of ten years they had paid everything, everything, with the rates of usury and the accumulations of the compound interest.

Madame Loisel looked old now. She had become the woman of impoverished households--strong and hard and rough. With frowsy hair, skirts askew and red hands, she talked loud while washing the floor with great swishes of water. But sometimes, when her husband was at the office, she sat down near the window and she thought of that gay evening of long ago, of that ball where she had been so beautiful and so admired.

What would have happened if she had not lost that necklace? Who knows? who knows? How strange and changeful is life! How small a thing is needed to make or ruin us!

But one Sunday, having gone to take a walk in the Champs Elysees to refresh herself after the labors of the week, she suddenly perceived a woman who was leading a child. It was Madame Forestier, still young, still beautiful, still charming.

Madame Loisel felt moved. Should she speak to her? Yes, certainly. And now that she had paid, she would tell her all about it. Why not?

She went up.

"Good-day, Jeanne."

The other, astonished to be familiarly addressed by this plain good-wife, did not recognize her at all and stammered:

"But--madame!--I do not know--You must have mistaken."

"No. I am Mathilde Loisel."

Her friend uttered a cry.

"Oh, my poor Mathilde! How you are changed!"

"Yes, I have had a pretty hard life, since I last saw you, and great poverty--and that because of you!"

"Of me! How so?"

"Do you remember that diamond necklace you lent me to wear at the ministerial ball?"

"Yes. Well?"

"Well, I lost it."

"What do you mean? You brought it back."

"I brought you back another exactly like it. And it has taken us ten years to pay for it. You can understand that it was not easy for us, for us who had nothing. At last it is ended, and I am very glad."

Madame Forestier had stopped.

"You say that you bought a necklace of diamonds to replace mine?"

"Yes. You never noticed it, then! They were very similar."

And she smiled with a joy that was at once proud and ingenuous.

Madame Forestier, deeply moved, took her hands.

"Oh, my poor Mathilde! Why, my necklace was paste! It was worth at most only five hundred francs!"

MADEMOISELLE FIFI

Major Graf Von Farlsberg, the Prussian commandant, was reading his newspaper as he lay back in a great easy-chair, with his booted feet on the beautiful marble mantelpiece where his spurs had made two holes, which had grown deeper every day during the three months that he had been in the chateau of Uville.

A cup of coffee was smoking on a small inlaid table, which was stained with liqueur, burned by cigars, notched by the penknife of the victorious officer, who occasionally would stop while sharpening a pencil, to jot down figures, or to make a drawing on it, just as it took his fancy.

When he had read his letters and the German newspapers, which his orderly had brought him, he got up, and after throwing three or four enormous pieces of green wood on the fire, for these gentlemen were gradually cutting down the park in order to keep themselves warm, he went to the window. The rain was descending in torrents, a regular Normandy rain, which looked as if it were being poured out by some furious person, a slanting rain, opaque as a curtain, which formed a kind of wall with diagonal stripes, and which deluged everything, a rain such as one frequently experiences in the neighborhood of Rouen, which is the watering-pot of France.

For a long time the officer looked at the sodden turf and at the swollen Andelle beyond it, which was overflowing its banks; he was drumming a waltz with his fingers on the window-panes, when a noise made him turn round. It was his second in command, Captain Baron van Kelweinstein.

The major was a giant, with broad shoulders and a long, fan-like beard, which hung down like a curtain to his chest. His whole solemn person suggested the idea of a military peacock, a peacock who was carrying his tail spread out on his breast. He had cold, gentle blue eyes, and a scar from a swordcut, which he had received in the war with Austria; he was said to be an honorable man, as well as a brave officer.

The captain, a short, red-faced man, was tightly belted in at the waist, his red hair was cropped quite close to his head, and in certain lights he almost looked as if he had been rubbed over with phosphorus. He had lost two front teeth one night, though he could not quite remember how, and this sometimes made him speak unintelligibly, and he had a bald patch on top of his head surrounded by a fringe of curly, bright golden hair, which made him look like a monk.

The commandant shook hands with him and drank his cup of coffee (the sixth that morning), while he listened to his subordinate's report of what had occurred; and then they both went to the window and declared that it was a very unpleasant outlook. The major, who was a quiet man, with a wife at home, could accommodate himself to everything; but the captain, who led a fast life, who was in the habit of frequenting low resorts, and enjoying women's society, was angry at having to be shut up for three months in that wretched hole.

There was a knock at the door, and when the commandant said, "Come in," one of the orderlies appeared, and by his mere presence announced that breakfast was ready. In the dining-room they met three other officers of lower rank--a lieutenant, Otto von Grossling, and two sub-lieutenants, Fritz Scheuneberg and Baron von Eyrick, a very short, fair-haired man, who was proud and brutal toward men, harsh toward prisoners and as explosive as gunpowder.

Since he had been in France his comrades had called him nothing but Mademoiselle Fifi. They had given him that nickname on account of his dandified style and small waist, which looked as if he wore corsets; of his pale face, on which his budding mustache scarcely showed, and on account of the habit he had acquired of employing the French expression, 'Fi, fi donc', which he pronounced with a slight whistle when he wished to express his sovereign contempt for persons or things.

The dining-room of the chateau was a magnificent long room, whose fine old mirrors, that were cracked by pistol bullets, and whose Flemish tapestry, which was cut to ribbons, and hanging in rags in places from sword-cuts, told too well what Mademoiselle Fifi's occupation was during his spare time.

There were three family portraits on the walls a steel-clad knight, a cardinal and a judge, who were all smoking long porcelain pipes, which had been inserted into holes in the canvas, while a lady in a long, pointed waist proudly exhibited a pair of enormous mustaches, drawn with charcoal. The officers ate their breakfast almost in silence in that mutilated room, which looked dull in the rain and melancholy in its dilapidated condition, although its old oak floor had become as solid as the stone floor of an inn.

When they had finished eating and were smoking and drinking, they began, as usual, to berate the dull life they were leading. The bottles of brandy and of liqueur passed from hand to hand, and all sat back in their chairs and took repeated sips from their glasses, scarcely removing from their mouths the long, curved stems, which terminated in china bowls, painted in a manner to delight a Hottentot.

As soon as their glasses were empty they filled them again, with a gesture of resigned weariness, but Mademoiselle Fifi emptied his every minute, and a soldier immediately gave him another. They were enveloped in a cloud of strong tobacco smoke, and seemed to be sunk in a state of drowsy, stupid intoxication, that condition of stupid intoxication of men who have nothing to do, when suddenly the baron sat up and said: "Heavens! This cannot go on; we must think of something to do." And on hearing this, Lieutenant Otto and Sub-lieutenant Fritz, who preeminently possessed the serious, heavy German countenance, said: "What, captain?"

He thought for a few moments and then replied: "What? Why, we must get up some entertainment, if the commandant will allow us." "What sort of an entertainment, captain?" the major asked, taking his pipe out of his mouth. "I will arrange all that, commandant," the baron said. "I will send Le Devoir to Rouen, and he will bring back some ladies. I know where they can be found, We will have supper here, as all the materials are at hand and; at least, we shall have a jolly evening."

Graf von Farlsberg shrugged his shoulders with a smile: "You must surely be mad, my friend."

But all the other officers had risen and surrounded their chief, saying: "Let the captain have his way, commandant; it is terribly dull here." And the major ended by yielding. "Very well," he replied, and the baron immediately sent for Le Devoir. He was an old non-commissioned officer, who had never been seen to smile, but who carried out all the orders of his superiors to the letter, no matter what they might be. He stood there, with an impassive face, while he received the baron's instructions, and then went out, and five minutes later a large military wagon, covered with tarpaulin, galloped off as fast as four horses could draw it in the pouring rain. The officers all seemed to awaken from their lethargy, their looks brightened, and they began to talk.

17

Although it was raining as hard as ever, the major declared that it was not so dark, and Lieutenant von Grossling said with conviction that the sky was clearing up, while Mademoiselle Fifi did not seem to be able to keep still. He got up and sat down again, and his bright eyes seemed to be looking for something to destroy. Suddenly, looking at the lady with the mustaches, the young fellow pulled out his revolver and said: "You shall not see it." And without leaving his seat he aimed, and with two successive bullets cut out both the eyes of the portrait.

"Let us make a mine!" he then exclaimed, and the conversation was suddenly interrupted, as if they had found some fresh and powerful subject of interest. The mine was his invention, his method of destruction, and his favorite amusement.

When he left the chateau, the lawful owner, Comte Fernand d'Amoys d'Uville, had not had time to carry away or to hide anything except the plate, which had been stowed away in a hole made in one of the walls. As he was very rich and had good taste, the large drawing-room, which opened into the dining-room, looked like a gallery in a museum, before his precipitate flight.

Expensive oil paintings, water colors and drawings hung against the walls, while on the tables, on the hanging shelves and in elegant glass cupboards there were a thousand ornaments: small vases, statuettes, groups of Dresden china and grotesque Chinese figures, old ivory and Venetian glass, which filled the large room with their costly and fantastic array.

Scarcely anything was left now; not that the things had been stolen, for the major would not have allowed that, but Mademoiselle Fifi would every now and then have a mine, and on those occasions all the officers thoroughly enjoyed themselves for five minutes. The little marquis went into the drawing-room to get what he wanted, and he brought back a small, delicate china teapot, which he filled with gunpowder, and carefully introduced a piece of punk through the spout. This he lighted and took his infernal machine into the next room, but he came back immediately and shut the door. The Germans all stood expectant, their faces full of childish, smiling curiosity, and as soon as the explosion had shaken the chateau, they all rushed in at once.

Mademoiselle Fifi, who got in first, clapped his hands in delight at the sight of a terra-cotta Venus, whose head had been blown off, and each picked up pieces of porcelain and wondered at the strange shape of the fragments, while the major was looking with a paternal eye at the large drawing-room, which had been wrecked after the fashion of a Nero, and was strewn with the fragments of works of art. He went out first and said with a smile: "That was a great success this time."

But there was such a cloud of smoke in the dining-room, mingled with the tobacco smoke, that they could not breathe, so the commandant opened the window, and all the officers, who had returned for a last glass of cognac, went up to it.

The moist air blew into the room, bringing with it a sort of powdery spray, which sprinkled their beards. They looked at the tall trees which were dripping with rain, at the broad valley which was covered with mist, and at the church spire in the distance, which rose up like a gray point in the beating rain.

The bells had not rung since their arrival. That was the only resistance which the invaders had met with in the neighborhood. The parish priest had not refused to take in and to feed the Prussian soldiers; he had several times even drunk a bottle of beer or claret with the hostile commandant, who often employed him as a benevolent intermediary; but it was no use to ask him for a single stroke of the bells; he would sooner have allowed himself to be shot. That was his way of protesting against the invasion, a peaceful and silent protest, the only one, he said, which was suitable to a priest, who was a man of mildness, and not of blood; and every one, for twenty-five miles round, praised Abbe Chantavoine's firmness and heroism in venturing to proclaim the public mourning by the obstinate silence of his church bells.

The whole village, enthusiastic at his resistance, was ready to back up their pastor and to risk anything, for they looked upon that silent protest as the safeguard of the national honor. It seemed to the peasants that thus they deserved better of their country than Belfort and Strassburg, that they had set an equally valuable example, and that the name of their little village would become immortalized by that; but, with that exception, they refused their Prussian conquerors nothing.

The commandant and his officers laughed among themselves at this inoffensive courage, and as the people in the whole country round showed themselves obliging and compliant toward them, they willingly tolerated their silent patriotism. Little Baron Wilhelm alone would have liked to have forced them to ring the bells. He was very angry at his superior's politic compliance with the priest's scruples, and every day begged the commandant to allow him to sound "ding-dong, ding-dong," just once, only just once, just by way of a joke. And he asked it in the coaxing, tender voice of some loved woman who is bent on obtaining her wish, but the commandant would not yield, and to console himself, Mademoiselle Fifi made a mine in the Chateau d'Uville.

The five men stood there together for five minutes, breathing in the moist air, and at last Lieutenant Fritz said with a laugh: "The ladies will certainly not have fine weather for their drive." Then they separated, each to his duty, while the captain had plenty to do in arranging for the dinner.

When they met again toward evening they began to laugh at seeing each other as spick and span and smart as on the day of a grand review. The commandant's hair did not look so gray as it was in the morning, and the captain had shaved, leaving only his mustache, which made him look as if he had a streak of fire under his nose.

In spite of the rain, they left the window open, and one of them went to listen from time to time; and at a quarter past six the baron said he heard a rumbling in the distance. They all rushed down, and presently the wagon drove up at a gallop with its four horses steaming and blowing, and splashed with mud to their girths. Five women dismounted, five handsome girls whom a comrade of the captain, to whom Le Devoir had presented his card, had selected with care.

They had not required much pressing, as they had got to know the Prussians in the three months during which they had had to do with them, and so they resigned themselves to the men as they did to the state of affairs.

They went at once into the dining-room, which looked still more dismal in its dilapidated condition when it was lighted up; while the table covered with choice dishes, the beautiful china and glass, and the plate, which had been found in the hole in the wall where its owner had hidden it, gave it the appearance of a bandits' inn, where they were supping after committing a robbery in the place. The captain was radiant, and put his arm round the women as if he were familiar with them; and when the three young men wanted to appropriate one each, he opposed them authoritatively, reserving to himself the right to apportion them justly, according to their several ranks, so as not to offend the higher powers. Therefore, to avoid all discussion, jarring, and suspicion of partiality, he placed them all in a row according to height, and addressing the tallest, he said in a voice of command:

"What is your name?" "Pamela," she replied, raising her voice. And then he said: "Number One, called Pamela, is adjudged to the commandant." Then,

20

having kissed Blondina, the second, as a sign of proprietorship, he proffered stout Amanda to Lieutenant Otto; Eva, "the Tomato," to Sub- lieutenant Fritz, and Rachel, the shortest of them all, a very young, dark girl, with eyes as black as ink, a Jewess, whose snub nose proved the rule which allots hooked noses to all her race, to the youngest officer, frail Count Wilhelm d'Eyrick.

They were all pretty and plump, without any distinctive features, and all had a similarity of complexion and figure.

The three young men wished to carry off their prizes immediately, under the pretext that they might wish to freshen their toilets; but the captain wisely opposed this, for he said they were quite fit to sit down to dinner, and his experience in such matters carried the day. There were only many kisses, expectant kisses.

Suddenly Rachel choked, and began to cough until the tears came into her eyes, while smoke came through her nostrils. Under pretence of kissing her, the count had blown a whiff of tobacco into her mouth. She did not fly into a rage and did not say a word, but she looked at her tormentor with latent hatred in her dark eyes.

They sat down to dinner. The commandant seemed delighted; he made Pamela sit on his right, and Blondina on his left, and said, as he unfolded his table napkin: "That was a delightful idea of yours, captain."

Lieutenants Otto and Fritz, who were as polite as if they had been with fashionable ladies, rather intimidated their guests, but Baron von Kelweinstein beamed, made obscene remarks and seemed on fire with his crown of red hair. He paid the women compliments in French of the Rhine, and sputtered out gallant remarks, only fit for a low pothouse, from between his two broken teeth.

They did not understand him, however, and their intelligence did not seem to be awakened until he uttered foul words and broad expressions, which were mangled by his accent. Then they all began to laugh at once like crazy women and fell against each other, repeating the words, which the baron then began to say all wrong, in order that he might have the pleasure of hearing them say dirty things. They gave him as much of that stuff as he wanted, for they were drunk after the first bottle of wine, and resuming their usual habits and manners, they kissed the officers to right and left of them, pinched their arms, uttered wild cries, drank out of every glass and sang French couplets and bits of German songs which they had picked up in their daily intercourse with the enemy.

Soon the men themselves became very unrestrained, shouted and broke the plates and dishes, while the soldiers behind them waited on them stolidly. The commandant was the only one who kept any restraint upon himself.

Mademoiselle Fifi had taken Rachel on his knee, and, getting excited, at one moment he kissed the little black curls on her neck and at another he pinched her furiously and made her scream, for he was seized by a species of ferocity, and tormented by his desire to hurt her. He often held her close to him and pressed a long kiss on the Jewess' rosy mouth until she lost her breath, and at last he bit her until a stream of blood ran down her chin and on to her bodice.

For the second time she looked him full in the face, and as she bathed the wound, she said: "You will have to pay for, that!" But he merely laughed a hard laugh and said: "I will pay."

At dessert champagne was served, and the commandant rose, and in the same voice in which he would have drunk to the health of the Empress Augusta, he drank: "To our ladies!" And a series of toasts began, toasts worthy of the lowest soldiers and of drunkards, mingled with obscene jokes, which were made still more brutal by their ignorance of the language. They got up, one after the other, trying to say something witty, forcing themselves to be funny, and the women, who were so drunk that they almost fell off their chairs, with vacant looks and clammy tongues applauded madly each time.

The captain, who no doubt wished to impart an appearance of gallantry to the orgy, raised his glass again and said: "To our victories over hearts." and, thereupon Lieutenant Otto, who was a species of bear from the Black Forest, jumped up, inflamed and saturated with drink, and suddenly seized by an access of alcoholic patriotism, he cried: "To our victories over France!"

Drunk as they were, the women were silent, but Rachel turned round, trembling, and said: "See here, I know some Frenchmen in whose presence you would not dare say that." But the little count, still holding her on his knee, began to laugh, for the wine had made him very merry, and said: "Ha! ha! ha! I have never met any of them myself. As soon as we show ourselves, they run away!" The girl, who was in a terrible rage, shouted into his face: "You are lying, you dirty scoundrel!"

For a moment he looked at her steadily with his bright eyes upon her, as he had looked at the portrait before he destroyed it with bullets from his revolver, and then he began to laugh: "Ah! yes, talk about them, my dear! Should we be here now if they were brave?" And, getting excited, he exclaimed: "We are the masters! France belongs to us!" She made one spring from his knee and threw herself into her chair, while he arose, held out his glass over the table and repeated: "France and the French, the woods, the fields and the houses of France belong to us!"

The others, who were quite drunk, and who were suddenly seized by military enthusiasm, the enthusiasm of brutes, seized their glasses, and shouting, "Long live Prussia!" they emptied them at a draught.

The girls did not protest, for they were reduced to silence and were afraid. Even Rachel did not say a word, as she had no reply to make. Then the little marquis put his champagne glass, which had just been refilled, on the head of the Jewess and exclaimed: "All the women in France belong to us also!"

At that she got up so quickly that the glass upset, spilling the amber- colored wine on her black hair as if to baptize her, and broke into a hundred fragments, as it fell to the floor. Her lips trembling, she defied the looks of the officer, who was still laughing, and stammered out in a voice choked with rage:

"That--that--that--is not true--for you shall not have the women of France!"

He sat down again so as to laugh at his ease; and, trying to speak with the Parisian accent, he said: "She is good, very good! Then why did you come here, my dear?" She was thunderstruck and made no reply for a moment, for in her agitation she did not understand him at first, but as soon as she grasped his meaning she said to him indignantly and vehemently: "I! I! I am not a woman, I am only a strumpet, and that is all that Prussians want."

Almost before she had finished he slapped her full in the face; but as he was raising his hand again, as if to strike her, she seized a small dessert knife with a silver blade from the table and, almost mad with rage, stabbed him right in the hollow of his neck. Something that he was going to say was cut short in his throat, and he sat there with his mouth half open and a terrible look in his eyes.

All the officers shouted in horror and leaped up tumultuously; but, throwing her chair between the legs of Lieutenant Otto, who fell down at full length, she

23

ran to the window, opened it before they could seize her and jumped out into the night and the pouring rain.

In two minutes Mademoiselle Fifi was dead, and Fritz and Otto drew their swords and wanted to kill the women, who threw themselves at their feet and clung to their knees. With some difficulty the major stopped the slaughter and had the four terrified girls locked up in a room under the care of two soldiers, and then he organized the pursuit of the fugitive as carefully as if he were about to engage in a skirmish, feeling quite sure that she would be caught.

The table, which had been cleared immediately, now served as a bed on which to lay out the lieutenant, and the four officers stood at the windows, rigid and sobered with the stern faces of soldiers on duty, and tried to pierce through the darkness of the night amid the steady torrent of rain. Suddenly a shot was heard and then another, a long way off; and for four hours they heard from time to time near or distant reports and rallying cries, strange words of challenge, uttered in guttural voices.

In the morning they all returned. Two soldiers had been killed and three others wounded by their comrades in the ardor of that chase and in the confusion of that nocturnal pursuit, but they had not caught Rachel.

Then the inhabitants of the district were terrorized, the houses were turned topsy-turvy, the country was scoured and beaten up, over and over again, but the Jewess did not seem to have left a single trace of her passage behind her.

When the general was told of it he gave orders to hush up the affair, so as not to set a bad example to the army, but he severely censured the commandant, who in turn punished his inferiors. The general had said: "One does not go to war in order to amuse one's self and to caress prostitutes." Graf von Farlsberg, in his exasperation, made up his mind to have his revenge on the district, but as he required a pretext for showing severity, he sent for the priest and ordered him to have the bell tolled at the funeral of Baron von Eyrick.

Contrary to all expectation, the priest showed himself humble and most respectful, and when Mademoiselle Fifi's body left the Chateau d'Uville on its way to the cemetery, carried by soldiers, preceded, surrounded and followed by soldiers who marched with loaded rifles, for the first time the bell sounded its funeral knell in a lively manner, as if a friendly hand were caressing it. At night it rang again, and the next day, and every day; it rang as much as any one could desire. Sometimes even it would start at night and sound gently through the

24

darkness, seized with a strange joy, awakened one could not tell why. All the peasants in the neighborhood declared that it was bewitched, and nobody except the priest and the sacristan would now go near the church tower. And they went because a poor girl was living there in grief and solitude and provided for secretly by those two men.

She remained there until the German troops departed, and then one evening the priest borrowed the baker's cart and himself drove his prisoner to Rouen. When they got there he embraced her, and she quickly went back on foot to the establishment from which she had come, where the proprietress, who thought that she was dead, was very glad to see her.

A short time afterward a patriot who had no prejudices, and who liked her because of her bold deed, and who afterward loved her for herself, married her and made her a lady quite as good as many others.

THE PIECE OF STRING

It was market-day, and from all the country round Goderville the peasants and their wives were coming toward the town. The men walked slowly, throwing the whole body forward at every step of their long, crooked legs. They were deformed from pushing the plough which makes the left- shoulder higher, and bends their figures side-ways; from reaping the grain, when they have to spread their legs so as to keep on their feet. Their starched blue blouses, glossy as though varnished, ornamented at collar and cuffs with a little embroidered design and blown out around their bony bodies, looked very much like balloons about to soar, whence issued two arms and two feet.

Some of these fellows dragged a cow or a calf at the end of a rope. And just behind the animal followed their wives beating it over the back with a leaf-covered branch to hasten its pace, and carrying large baskets out of which protruded the heads of chickens or ducks. These women walked more quickly and energetically than the men, with their erect, dried-up figures, adorned with scanty little shawls pinned over their flat bosoms, and their heads wrapped round with a white cloth, enclosing the hair and surmounted by a cap.

Now a char-a-banc passed by, jogging along behind a nag and shaking up strangely the two men on the seat, and the woman at the bottom of the cart who held fast to its sides to lessen the hard jolting.

In the market-place at Goderville was a great crowd, a mingled multitude of men and beasts. The horns of cattle, the high, long-napped hats of wealthy peasants, the headdresses of the women came to the surface of that sea. And the sharp, shrill, barking voices made a continuous, wild din, while above it occasionally rose a huge burst of laughter from the sturdy lungs of a merry peasant or a prolonged bellow from a cow tied fast to the wall of a house.

It all smelled of the stable, of milk, of hay and of perspiration, giving off that half-human, half-animal odor which is peculiar to country folks.

Maitre Hauchecorne, of Breaute, had just arrived at Goderville and was making his way toward the square when he perceived on the ground a little piece of string. Maitre Hauchecorne, economical as are all true Normans, reflected that everything was worth picking up which could be of any use, and he stooped down, but painfully, because he suffered from rheumatism. He took the bit of thin string from the ground and was carefully preparing to roll it up when he saw Maitre Malandain, the harness maker, on his doorstep staring at him. They had once had a quarrel about a halter, and they had borne each other malice ever since. Maitre Hauchecorne was overcome with a sort of shame at being seen by his enemy picking up a bit of string in the road. He quickly hid it beneath his blouse and then slipped it into his breeches, pocket, then pretended to be still looking for something on the ground which he did not discover and finally went off toward the market-place, his head bent forward and his body almost doubled in two by rheumatic pains.

He was at once lost in the crowd, which kept moving about slowly and noisily as it chaffered and bargained. The peasants examined the cows, went off, came back, always in doubt for fear of being cheated, never quite daring to decide, looking the seller square in the eye in the effort to discover the tricks of the man and the defect in the beast.

The women, having placed their great baskets at their feet, had taken out the poultry, which lay upon the ground, their legs tied together, with terrified eyes and scarlet combs.

They listened to propositions, maintaining their prices in a decided manner with an impassive face or perhaps deciding to accept the smaller price offered, suddenly calling out to the customer who was starting to go away:

"All right, I'll let you have them, Mait' Anthime."

Then, little by little, the square became empty, and when the Angelus struck midday those who lived at a distance poured into the inns.

At Jourdain's the great room was filled with eaters, just as the vast court was filled with vehicles of every sort--wagons, gigs, chars-a- bancs, tilburies, innumerable vehicles which have no name, yellow with mud, misshapen, pieced together, raising their shafts to heaven like two arms, or it may be with their nose on the ground and their rear in the air.

Just opposite to where the diners were at table the huge fireplace, with its bright flame, gave out a burning heat on the backs of those who sat at the right. Three spits were turning, loaded with chickens, with pigeons and with joints of mutton, and a delectable odor of roast meat and of gravy flowing over crisp brown skin arose from the hearth, kindled merriment, caused mouths to water.

All the aristocracy of the plough were eating there at Mait' Jourdain's, the innkeeper's, a dealer in horses also and a sharp fellow who had made a great deal of money in his day.

The dishes were passed round, were emptied, as were the jugs of yellow cider. Every one told of his affairs, of his purchases and his sales. They exchanged news about the crops. The weather was good for greens, but too wet for grain.

Suddenly the drum began to beat in the courtyard before the house. Every one, except some of the most indifferent, was on their feet at once and ran to the door, to the windows, their mouths full and napkins in their hand.

When the public crier had finished his tattoo he called forth in a jerky voice, pausing in the wrong places:

"Be it known to the inhabitants of Goderville and in general to all persons present at the market that there has been lost this morning on the Beuzeville road, between nine and ten o'clock, a black leather pocketbook containing five hundred francs and business papers. You are requested to return it to the mayor's office at once or to Maitre Fortune Houlbreque, of Manneville. There will be twenty francs reward."

Then the man went away. They heard once more at a distance the dull beating of the drum and the faint voice of the crier. Then they all began to talk of this incident, reckoning up the chances which Maitre Houlbreque had of finding or of not finding his pocketbook again.

The meal went on. They were finishing their coffee when the corporal of gendarmes appeared on the threshold.

He asked:

"Is Maitre Hauchecorne, of Breaute, here?"

Maitre Hauchecorne, seated at the other end of the table answered:

"Here I am, here I am."

And he followed the corporal.

The mayor was waiting for him, seated in an armchair. He was the notary of the place, a tall, grave man of pompous speech.

"Maitre Hauchecorne," said he, "this morning on the Beuzeville road, you were seen to pick up the pocketbook lost by Maitre Houlbreque, of Manneville."

The countryman looked at the mayor in amazement frightened already at this suspicion which rested on him, he knew not why.

"I--I picked up that pocketbook?"

"Yes, YOU."

"I swear I don't even know anything about it."

"You were seen."

"I was seen--I? Who saw me?"

"M. Malandain, the harness-maker."

Then the old man remembered, understood, and, reddening with anger, said:

"Ah! he saw me, did he, the rascal? He saw me picking up this string here, M'sieu le Maire."

And fumbling at the bottom of his pocket, he pulled out of it the little end of string.

But the mayor incredulously shook his head:

"You will not make me believe, Maitre Hauchecorne, that M. Malandain, who is a man whose word can be relied on, has mistaken this string for a pocketbook."

The peasant, furious, raised his hand and spat on the ground beside him as if to attest his good faith, repeating:

"For all that, it is God's truth, M'sieu le Maire. There! On my soul's salvation, I repeat it."

The mayor continued:

"After you picked up the object in question, you even looked about for some time in the mud to see if a piece of money had not dropped out of it."

The good man was choking with indignation and fear.

"How can they tell--how can they tell such lies as that to slander an honest man! How can they?"

His protestations were in vain; he was not believed.

He was confronted with M. Malandain, who repeated and sustained his testimony. They railed at one another for an hour. At his own request Maitre Hauchecorne was searched. Nothing was found on him.

At last the mayor, much perplexed, sent him away, warning him that he would inform the public prosecutor and ask for orders.

The news had spread. When he left the mayor's office the old man was surrounded, interrogated with a curiosity which was serious or mocking, as the case might be, but into which no indignation entered. And he began to tell the story of the string. They did not believe him. They laughed.

He passed on, buttonholed by every one, himself buttonholing his acquaintances, beginning over and over again his tale and his protestations, showing his pockets turned inside out to prove that he had nothing in them.

They said to him:

"You old rogue!"

He grew more and more angry, feverish, in despair at not being believed, and kept on telling his story.

The night came. It was time to go home. He left with three of his neighbors, to whom he pointed out the place where he had picked up the string, and all the way he talked of his adventure.

That evening he made the round of the village of Breaute for the purpose of telling every one. He met only unbelievers.

He brooded over it all night long.

The next day, about one in the afternoon, Marius Paumelle, a farm hand of Maitre Breton, the market gardener at Ymauville, returned the pocketbook and its contents to Maitre Holbreque, of Manneville.

This man said, indeed, that he had found it on the road, but not knowing how to read, he had carried it home and given it to his master.

The news spread to the environs. Maitre Hauchecorne was informed. He started off at once and began to relate his story with the denoument. He was triumphant.

"What grieved me," said he, "was not the thing itself, do you understand, but it was being accused of lying. Nothing does you so much harm as being in disgrace for lying."

All day he talked of his adventure. He told it on the roads to the people who passed, at the cabaret to the people who drank and next Sunday when they came out of church. He even stopped strangers to tell them about it. He was easy now, and yet something worried him without his knowing exactly what it was. People had a joking manner while they listened. They did not seem convinced. He seemed to feel their remarks behind his back.

On Tuesday of the following week he went to market at Goderville, prompted solely by the need of telling his story.

Malandain, standing on his doorstep, began to laugh as he saw him pass. Why?

He accosted a farmer of Criquetot, who did not let hire finish, and giving him a punch in the pit of the stomach cried in his face: "Oh, you great rogue!" Then he turned his heel upon him.

Maitre Hauchecorne remained speechless and grew more and more uneasy. Why had they called him "great rogue"?

When seated at table in Jourdain's tavern he began again to explain the whole affair.

A horse dealer of Montivilliers shouted at him:

"Get out, get out, you old scamp! I know all about your old string."

Hauchecorne stammered:

"But since they found it again, the pocketbook!"

But the other continued:

"Hold your tongue, daddy; there's one who finds it and there's another who returns it. And no one the wiser."

The farmer was speechless. He understood at last. They accused him of having had the pocketbook brought back by an accomplice, by a confederate.

He tried to protest. The whole table began to laugh.

He could not finish his dinner, and went away amid a chorus of jeers.

He went home indignant, choking with rage, with confusion, the more cast down since with his Norman craftiness he was, perhaps, capable of having done what they accused him of and even of boasting of it as a good trick. He was dimly conscious that it was impossible to prove his innocence, his craftiness being so well known. He felt himself struck to the heart by the injustice of the suspicion.

He began anew to tell his tale, lengthening his recital every day, each day adding new proofs, more energetic declarations and more sacred oaths, which he thought of, which he prepared in his hours of solitude, for his mind was entirely occupied with the story of the string. The more he denied it, the more artful his arguments, the less he was believed.

"Those are liars proofs," they said behind his back.

He felt this. It preyed upon him and he exhausted himself in useless efforts.

He was visibly wasting away.

Jokers would make him tell the story of "the piece of string" to amuse them, just as you make a soldier who has been on a campaign tell his story of the battle. His mind kept growing weaker and about the end of December he took to his bed.

He passed away early in January, and, in the ravings of death agony, he protested his innocence, repeating:

"A little bit of string--a little bit of string. See, here it is, M'sieu le Maire."

TWO FRIENDS

Besieged Paris was in the throes of famine. Even the sparrows on the roofs and the rats in the sewers were growing scarce. People were eating anything they could get.

As Monsieur Morissot, watchmaker by profession and idler for the nonce, was strolling along the boulevard one bright January morning, his hands in his trousers pockets and stomach empty, he suddenly came face to face with an acquaintance--Monsieur Sauvage, a fishing chum.

Before the war broke out Morissot had been in the habit, every Sunday morning, of setting forth with a bamboo rod in his hand and a tin box on his back. He took the Argenteuil train, got out at Colombes, and walked thence to the Ile Marante. The moment he arrived at this place of his dreams he began fishing, and fished till nightfall.

Every Sunday he met in this very spot Monsieur Sauvage, a stout, jolly, little man, a draper in the Rue Notre Dame de Lorette, and also an ardent fisherman. They often spent half the day side by side, rod in hand and feet dangling over the water, and a warm friendship had sprung up between the two.

Some days they did not speak; at other times they chatted; but they understood each other perfectly without the aid of words, having similar tastes and feelings.

In the spring, about ten o'clock in the morning, when the early sun caused a light mist to float on the water and gently warmed the backs of the two enthusiastic anglers, Morissot would occasionally remark to his neighbor:

"My, but it's pleasant here."

To which the other would reply:

"I can't imagine anything better!"

And these few words sufficed to make them understand and appreciate each other.

In the autumn, toward the close of day, when the setting sun shed a blood-red glow over the western sky, and the reflection of the crimson clouds tinged the whole river with red, brought a glow to the faces of the two friends, and gilded the trees, whose leaves were already turning at the first chill touch of winter, Monsieur Sauvage would sometimes smile at Morissot, and say:

"What a glorious spectacle!"

And Morissot would answer, without taking his eyes from his float:

"This is much better than the boulevard, isn't it?"

As soon as they recognized each other they shook hands cordially, affected at the thought of meeting under such changed circumstances.

Monsieur Sauvage, with a sigh, murmured:

"These are sad times!"

Morissot shook his head mournfully.

"And such weather! This is the first fine day of the year."

The sky was, in fact, of a bright, cloudless blue.

They walked along, side by side, reflective and sad.

"And to think of the fishing!" said Morissot. "What good times we used to have!"

"When shall we be able to fish again?" asked Monsieur Sauvage.

They entered a small cafe and took an absinthe together, then resumed their walk along the pavement.

Morissot stopped suddenly.

"Shall we have another absinthe?" he said.

"If you like," agreed Monsieur Sauvage.

And they entered another wine shop.

They were quite unsteady when they came out, owing to the effect of the alcohol on their empty stomachs. It was a fine, mild day, and a gentle breeze fanned their faces.

The fresh air completed the effect of the alcohol on Monsieur Sauvage. He stopped suddenly, saying:

"Suppose we go there?"

"Where?"

"Fishing."

"But where?"

"Why, to the old place. The French outposts are close to Colombes. I know Colonel Dumoulin, and we shall easily get leave to pass."

Morissot trembled with desire.

"Very well. I agree."

And they separated, to fetch their rods and lines.

An hour later they were walking side by side on the-highroad. Presently they reached the villa occupied by the colonel. He smiled at their request, and granted it. They resumed their walk, furnished with a password.

Soon they left the outposts behind them, made their way through deserted Colombes, and found themselves on the outskirts of the small vineyards which border the Seine. It was about eleven o'clock.

Before them lay the village of Argenteuil, apparently lifeless. The heights of Orgement and Sannois dominated the landscape. The great plain, extending as far as Nanterre, was empty, quite empty-a waste of dun-colored soil and bare cherry trees.

Monsieur Sauvage, pointing to the heights, murmured:

"The Prussians are up yonder!"

And the sight of the deserted country filled the two friends with vague misgivings.

The Prussians! They had never seen them as yet, but they had felt their presence in the neighborhood of Paris for months past--ruining France, pillaging, massacring, starving them. And a kind of superstitious terror mingled with the hatred they already felt toward this unknown, victorious nation.

"Suppose we were to meet any of them?" said Morissot.

"We'd offer them some fish," replied Monsieur Sauvage, with that Parisian light-heartedness which nothing can wholly quench.

Still, they hesitated to show themselves in the open country, overawed by the utter silence which reigned around them.

At last Monsieur Sauvage said boldly:

"Come, we'll make a start; only let us be careful!"

And they made their way through one of the vineyards, bent double, creeping along beneath the cover afforded by the vines, with eye and ear alert.

A strip of bare ground remained to be crossed before they could gain the river bank. They ran across this, and, as soon as they were at the water's edge, concealed themselves among the dry reeds.

Morissot placed his ear to the ground, to ascertain, if possible, whether footsteps were coming their way. He heard nothing. They seemed to be utterly alone.

Their confidence was restored, and they began to fish.

Before them the deserted Ile Marante hid them from the farther shore. The little restaurant was closed, and looked as if it had been deserted for years.

Monsieur Sauvage caught the first gudgeon, Monsieur Morissot the second, and almost every moment one or other raised his line with a little, glittering, silvery fish wriggling at the end; they were having excellent sport.

They slipped their catch gently into a close-meshed bag lying at their feet; they were filled with joy--the joy of once more indulging in a pastime of which they had long been deprived.

The sun poured its rays on their backs; they no longer heard anything or thought of anything. They ignored the rest of the world; they were fishing.

But suddenly a rumbling sound, which seemed to come from the bowels of the earth, shook the ground beneath them: the cannon were resuming their thunder.

Morissot turned his head and could see toward the left, beyond the banks of the river, the formidable outline of Mont-Valerien, from whose summit arose a white puff of smoke.

The next instant a second puff followed the first, and in a few moments a fresh detonation made the earth tremble.

Others followed, and minute by minute the mountain gave forth its deadly breath and a white puff of smoke, which rose slowly into the peaceful heaven and floated above the summit of the cliff.

Monsieur Sauvage shrugged his shoulders.

"They are at it again!" he said.

Morissot, who was anxiously watching his float bobbing up and down, was suddenly seized with the angry impatience of a peaceful man toward the madmen who were firing thus, and remarked indignantly:

"What fools they are to kill one another like that!"

"They're worse than animals," replied Monsieur Sauvage.

And Morissot, who had just caught a bleak, declared:

"And to think that it will be just the same so long as there are governments!"

"The Republic would not have declared war," interposed Monsieur Sauvage.

Morissot interrupted him:

"Under a king we have foreign wars; under a republic we have civil war."

And the two began placidly discussing political problems with the sound common sense of peaceful, matter-of-fact citizens--agreeing on one point: that they would never be free. And Mont-Valerien thundered ceaselessly, demolishing the houses of the French with its cannon balls, grinding lives of men to powder, destroying many a dream, many a cherished hope, many a prospective happiness; ruthlessly causing endless woe and suffering in the hearts of wives, of daughters, of mothers, in other lands.

"Such is life!" declared Monsieur Sauvage.

"Say, rather, such is death!" replied Morissot, laughing.

But they suddenly trembled with alarm at the sound of footsteps behind them, and, turning round, they perceived close at hand four tall, bearded men, dressed after the manner of livery servants and wearing flat caps on their heads. They were covering the two anglers with their rifles.

The rods slipped from their owners' grasp and floated away down the river.

In the space of a few seconds they were seized, bound, thrown into a boat, and taken across to the Ile Marante.

And behind the house they had thought deserted were about a score of German soldiers.

A shaggy-looking giant, who was bestriding a chair and smoking a long clay pipe, addressed them in excellent French with the words:

"Well, gentlemen, have you had good luck with your fishing?"

Then a soldier deposited at the officer's feet the bag full of fish, which he had taken care to bring away. The Prussian smiled.

"Not bad, I see. But we have something else to talk about. Listen to me, and don't be alarmed:

"You must know that, in my eyes, you are two spies sent to reconnoitre me and my movements. Naturally, I capture you and I shoot you. You pretended to be fishing, the better to disguise your real errand. You have fallen into my hands, and must take the consequences. Such is war.

"But as you came here through the outposts you must have a password for your return. Tell me that password and I will let you go."

The two friends, pale as death, stood silently side by side, a slight fluttering of the hands alone betraying their emotion.

"No one will ever know," continued the officer. "You will return peacefully to your homes, and the secret will disappear with you. If you refuse, it means death-instant death. Choose!"

They stood motionless, and did not open their lips.

The Prussian, perfectly calm, went on, with hand outstretched toward the river:

"Just think that in five minutes you will be at the bottom of that water. In five minutes! You have relations, I presume?"

Mont-Valerien still thundered.

The two fishermen remained silent. The German turned and gave an order in his own language. Then he moved his chair a little way off, that he might not be so near the prisoners, and a dozen men stepped forward, rifle in hand, and took up a position, twenty paces off.

"I give you one minute," said the officer; "not a second longer."

Then he rose quickly, went over to the two Frenchmen, took Morissot by the arm, led him a short distance off, and said in a low voice:

"Quick! the password! Your friend will know nothing. I will pretend to relent."

Morissot answered not a word.

Then the Prussian took Monsieur Sauvage aside in like manner, and made him the same proposal.

Monsieur Sauvage made no reply.

Again they stood side by side.

The officer issued his orders; the soldiers raised their rifles.

Then by chance Morissot's eyes fell on the bag full of gudgeon lying in the grass a few feet from him.

A ray of sunlight made the still quivering fish glisten like silver. And Morissot's heart sank. Despite his efforts at self-control his eyes filled with tears.

"Good-by, Monsieur Sauvage," he faltered.

"Good-by, Monsieur Morissot," replied Sauvage.

They shook hands, trembling from head to foot with a dread beyond their mastery.

The officer cried:

"Fire!"

The twelve shots were as one.

Monsieur Sauvage fell forward instantaneously. Morissot, being the taller, swayed slightly and fell across his friend with face turned skyward and blood oozing from a rent in the breast of his coat.

The German issued fresh orders.

His men dispersed, and presently returned with ropes and large stones, which they attached to the feet of the two friends; then they carried them to the river bank.

Mont-Valerien, its summit now enshrouded in smoke, still continued to thunder.

Two soldiers took Morissot by the head and the feet; two others did the same with Sauvage. The bodies, swung lustily by strong hands, were cast to a distance, and, describing a curve, fell feet foremost into the stream.

The water splashed high, foamed, eddied, then grew calm; tiny waves lapped the shore.

A few streaks of blood flecked the surface of the river.

The officer, calm throughout, remarked, with grim humor:

"It's the fishes' turn now!"

Then he retraced his way to the house.

Suddenly he caught sight of the net full of gudgeons, lying forgotten in the grass. He picked it up, examined it, smiled, and called:

"Wilhelm!"

A white-aproned soldier responded to the summons, and the Prussian, tossing him the catch of the two murdered men, said:

"Have these fish fried for me at once, while they are still alive; they'll make a tasty dish."

Then he resumed his pipe.

MISS HARRIET

There were seven of us on a drag, four women and three men; one of the latter sat on the box seat beside the coachman. We were ascending, at a snail's pace, the winding road up the steep cliff along the coast.

Setting out from Etretat at break of day in order to visit the ruins of Tancarville, we were still half asleep, benumbed by the fresh air of the morning. The women especially, who were little accustomed to these early excursions, half opened and closed their eyes every moment, nodding their heads or yawning, quite insensible to the beauties of the dawn.

It was autumn. On both sides of the road stretched the bare fields, yellowed by the stubble of wheat and oats which covered the soil like a beard that had been badly shaved. The moist earth seemed to steam. Larks were singing high up in the air, while other birds piped in the bushes.

The sun rose at length in front of us, bright red on the plane of the horizon, and in proportion as it ascended, growing clearer from minute to minute, the country seemed to awake, to smile, to shake itself like a young girl leaving her bed in her white robe of vapor. The Comte d'Etraille, who was seated on the box, cried:

"Look! look! a hare!" and he extended his arm toward the left, pointing to a patch of clover. The animal scurried along, almost hidden by the clover, only its large ears showing. Then it swerved across a furrow, stopped, started off again at full speed, changed its course, stopped anew, uneasy, spying out every danger, uncertain what route to take, when suddenly it began to run with great bounds, disappearing finally in a large patch of beet-root. All the men had waked up to watch the course of the animal.

Rene Lamanoir exclaimed:

"We are not at all gallant this morning," and; regarding his neighbor, the little Baroness de Serennes, who struggled against sleep, he said to her in a low tone: "You are thinking of your husband, baroness. Reassure yourself; he will not return before Saturday, so you have still four days."

She answered with a sleepy smile:

"How stupid you are!" Then, shaking off her torpor, she added: "Now, let somebody say something to make us laugh. You, Monsieur Chenal, who have the reputation of having had more love affairs than the Due de Richelieu, tell us a love story in which you have played a part; anything you like."

Leon Chenal, an old painter, who had once been very handsome, very strong, very proud of his physique and very popular with women, took his long white beard in his hand and smiled. Then, after a few moments' reflection, he suddenly became serious.

"Ladies, it will not be an amusing tale, for I am going to relate to you the saddest love affair of my life, and I sincerely hope that none of my friends may ever pass through a similar experience.

"I was twenty-five years of age and was pillaging along the coast of Normandy. I call 'pillaging' wandering about, with a knapsack on one's back, from inn to inn, under the pretext of making studies and sketching landscapes. I knew nothing more enjoyable than that happy-go-lucky wandering life, in which one is perfectly free, without shackles of any kind, without care, without preoccupation, without thinking even of the morrow. One goes in any direction one pleases, without any guide save his fancy, without any counsellor save his eyes. One stops because a running brook attracts one, because the smell of potatoes frying tickles one's olfactories on passing an inn. Sometimes it is the perfume of clematis which decides one in his choice or the roguish glance of the servant at an inn. Do not despise me for my affection for these rustics. These girls have a soul as well as senses, not to mention firm cheeks and fresh lips; while their hearty and willing kisses have the flavor of wild fruit. Love is always love, come whence it may. A heart that beats at your approach, an eye that weeps when you go away are things so rare, so sweet, so precious that they must never be despised.

"I have had rendezvous in ditches full of primroses, behind the cow stable and in barns among the straw, still warm from the heat of the day. I have recollections of coarse gray cloth covering supple peasant skin and regrets for

45

simple, frank kisses, more delicate in their unaffected sincerity than the subtle favors of charming and distinguished women.

"But what one loves most amid all these varied adventures is the country, the woods, the rising of the sun, the twilight, the moonlight. These are, for the painter, honeymoon trips with Nature. One is alone with her in that long and quiet association. You go to sleep in the fields, amid marguerites and poppies, and when you open your eyes in the full glare of the sunlight you descry in the distance the little village with its pointed clock tower which sounds the hour of noon.

"You sit down by the side of a spring which gushes out at the foot of an oak, amid a growth of tall, slender weeds, glistening with life. You go down on your knees, bend forward and drink that cold, pellucid water which wets your mustache and nose; you drink it with a physical pleasure, as though you kissed the spring, lip to lip. Sometimes, when you find a deep hole along the course of these tiny brooks, you plunge in quite naked, and you feel on your skin, from head to foot, as it were, an icy and delicious caress, the light and gentle quivering of the stream.

"You are gay on the hills, melancholy on the edge of ponds, inspired when the sun is setting in an ocean of blood-red clouds and casts red reflections or the river. And at night, under the moon, which passes across the vault of heaven, you think of a thousand strange things which would never have occurred to your mind under the brilliant light of day.

"So, in wandering through the same country where we, are this year, I came to the little village of Benouville, on the cliff between Yport and Etretat. I came from Fecamp, following the coast, a high coast as straight as a wall, with its projecting chalk cliffs descending perpendicularly into the sea. I had walked since early morning on the short grass, smooth and yielding as a carpet, that grows on the edge of the cliff. And, singing lustily, I walked with long strides, looking sometimes at the slow circling flight of a gull with its white curved wings outlined on the blue sky, sometimes at the brown sails of a fishing bark on the green sea. In short, I had passed a happy day, a day of liberty and of freedom from care.

"A little farmhouse where travellers were lodged was pointed out to me, a kind of inn, kept by a peasant woman, which stood in the centre of a Norman courtyard surrounded by a double row of beeches.

"Leaving the coast, I reached the hamlet, which was hemmed in by great trees, and I presented myself at the house of Mother Lecacheur.

"She was an old, wrinkled and stern peasant woman, who seemed always to receive customers under protest, with a kind of defiance.

"It was the month of May. The spreading apple trees covered the court with a shower of blossoms which rained unceasingly both upon people and upon the grass.

"I said: 'Well, Madame Lecacheur, have you a room for me?'

"Astonished to find that I knew her name, she answered:

"'That depends; everything is let, but all the same I can find out."

"In five minutes we had come to an agreement, and I deposited my bag upon the earthen floor of a rustic room, furnished with a bed, two chairs, a table and a washbowl. The room looked into the large, smoky kitchen, where the lodgers took their meals with the people of the farm and the landlady, who was a widow.

"I washed my hands, after which I went out. The old woman was making a chicken fricassee for dinner in the large fireplace in which hung the iron pot, black with smoke.

"'You have travellers, then, at the present time?' said I to her.

"She answered in an offended tone of voice:

"'I have a lady, an English lady, who has reached years of maturity. She occupies the other room.'

"I obtained, by means of an extra five sous a day, the privilege of dining alone out in the yard when the weather was fine.

"My place was set outside the door, and I was beginning to gnaw the lean limbs of the Normandy chicken, to drink the clear cider and to munch the hunk of white bread, which was four days old but excellent.

"Suddenly the wooden gate which gave on the highway was opened, and a strange lady directed her steps toward the house. She was very thin, very tall, so tightly enveloped in a red Scotch plaid shawl that one might have supposed she had no arms, if one had not seen a long hand appear just above the hips, holding a white tourist umbrella. Her face was like that of a mummy, surrounded with curls of gray hair, which tossed about at every step she took and made me think, I know not why, of a pickled herring in curl papers. Lowering her eyes, she passed quickly in front of me and entered the house.

"That singular apparition cheered me. She undoubtedly was my neighbor, the English lady of mature age of whom our hostess had spoken.

"I did not see her again that day. The next day, when I had settled myself to commence painting at the end of that beautiful valley which you know and which extends as far as Etretat, I perceived, on lifting my eyes suddenly, something singular standing on the crest of the cliff, one might have said a pole decked out with flags. It was she. On seeing me, she suddenly disappeared. I reentered the house at midday for lunch and took my seat at the general table, so as to make the acquaintance of this odd character. But she did not respond to my polite advances, was insensible even to my little attentions. I poured out water for her persistently, I passed her the dishes with great eagerness. A slight, almost imperceptible, movement of the head and an English word, murmured so low that I did not understand it, were her only acknowledgments.

"I ceased occupying myself with her, although she had disturbed my thoughts.

"At the end of three days I knew as much about her as did Madame Lecacheur herself.

"She was called Miss Harriet. Seeking out a secluded village in which to pass the summer, she had been attracted to Benouville some six months before and did not seem disposed to leave it. She never spoke at table, ate rapidly, reading all the while a small book of the Protestant propaganda. She gave a copy of it to everybody. The cure himself had received no less than four copies, conveyed by an urchin to whom she had paid two sous commission. She said sometimes to our hostess abruptly, without preparing her in the least for the declaration:

"'I love the Saviour more than all. I admire him in all creation; I adore him in all nature; I carry him always in my heart.'

"And she would immediately present the old woman with one of her tracts which were destined to convert the universe.

"In, the village she was not liked. In fact, the schoolmaster having pronounced her an atheist, a kind of stigma attached to her. The cure, who had been consulted by Madame Lecacheur, responded:

"'She is a heretic, but God does not wish the death of the sinner, and I believe her to be a person of pure morals.'

"These words, 'atheist,' 'heretic,' words which no one can precisely define, threw doubts into some minds. It was asserted, however, that this English woman was rich and that she had passed her life in travelling through every country in the world because her family had cast her off. Why had her family cast her off? Because of her impiety, of course!

"She was, in fact, one of those people of exalted principles; one of those opinionated puritans, of which England produces so many; one of those good and insupportable old maids who haunt the tables d'hote of every hotel in Europe, who spoil Italy, poison Switzerland, render the charming cities of the Mediterranean uninhabitable, carry everywhere their fantastic manias their manners of petrified vestals, their indescribable toilets and a certain odor of india-rubber which makes one believe that at night they are slipped into a rubber casing.

"Whenever I caught sight of one of these individuals in a hotel I fled like the birds who see a scarecrow in a field.

"This woman, however, appeared so very singular that she did not displease me.

"Madame Lecacheur, hostile by instinct to everything that was not rustic, felt in her narrow soul a kind of hatred for the ecstatic declarations of the old maid. She had found a phrase by which to describe her, a term of contempt that rose to her lips, called forth by I know not what confused and mysterious mental ratiocination. She said: 'That woman is a demoniac.' This epithet, applied to that austere and sentimental creature, seemed to me irresistibly droll. I myself never called her anything now but 'the demoniac,' experiencing a singular pleasure in pronouncing aloud this word on perceiving her.

49

"One day I asked Mother Lecacheur: 'Well, what is our demoniac about to-day?'

"To which my rustic friend replied with a shocked air:

"'What do you think, sir? She picked up a toad which had had its paw crushed and carried it to her room and has put it in her washbasin and bandaged it as if it were a man. If that is not profanation I should like to know what is!'

"On another occasion, when walking along the shore she bought a large fish which had just been caught, simply to throw it back into the sea again. The sailor from whom she had bought it, although she paid him handsomely, now began to swear, more exasperated, indeed, than if she had put her hand into his pocket and taken his money. For more than a month he could not speak of the circumstance without becoming furious and denouncing it as an outrage. Oh, yes! She was indeed a demoniac, this Miss Harriet, and Mother Lecacheur must have had an inspiration in thus christening her.

"The stable boy, who was called Sapeur, because he had served in Africa in his youth, entertained other opinions. He said with a roguish air: 'She is an old hag who has seen life.'

"If the poor woman had but known!

"The little kind-hearted Celeste did not wait upon her willingly, but I was never able to understand why. Probably her only reason was that she was a stranger, of another race; of a different tongue and of another religion. She was, in fact, a demoniac!

"She passed her time wandering about the country, adoring and seeking God in nature. I found her one evening on her knees in a cluster of bushes. Having discovered something red through the leaves, I brushed aside the branches, and Miss Harriet at once rose to her feet, confused at having been found thus, fixing on me terrified eyes like those of an owl surprised in open day.

"Sometimes, when I was working among the rocks, I would suddenly descry her on the edge of the cliff like a lighthouse signal. She would be gazing in rapture at the vast sea glittering in the sunlight and the boundless sky with its golden tints. Sometimes I would distinguish her at the end of the valley, walking quickly with her elastic English step, and I would go toward her, attracted by I know not what, simply to see her illuminated visage, her dried-up, ineffable features, which seemed to glow with inward and profound happiness.

"I would often encounter her also in the corner of a field, sitting on the grass under the shadow of an apple tree, with her little religious booklet lying open on her knee while she gazed out at the distance.

"I could not tear myself away from that quiet country neighborhood, to which I was attached by a thousand links of love for its wide and peaceful landscape. I was happy in this sequestered farm, far removed from everything, but in touch with the earth, the good, beautiful, green earth. And--must I avow it?--there was, besides, a little curiosity which retained me at the residence of Mother Lecacheur. I wished to become acquainted a little with this strange Miss Harriet and to know what transpires in the solitary souls of those wandering old English women.

"We became acquainted in a rather singular manner. I had just finished a study which appeared to me to be worth something, and so it was, as it sold for ten thousand francs fifteen years later. It was as simple, however, as two and two make four and was not according to academic rules. The whole right side of my canvas represented a rock, an enormous rock, covered with sea-wrack, brown, yellow and red, across which the sun poured like a stream of oil. The light fell upon the rock as though it were aflame without the sun, which was at my back, being visible. That was all. A first bewildering study of blazing, gorgeous light.

"On the left was the sea, not the blue sea, the slate-colored sea, but a sea of jade, greenish, milky and solid beneath the deep-colored sky.

"I was so pleased with my work that I danced from sheer delight as I carried it back to the inn. I would have liked the whole world to see it at once. I can remember that I showed it to a cow that was browsing by the wayside, exclaiming as I did so: 'Look at that, my old beauty; you will not often see its like again.'

"When I had reached the house I immediately called out to Mother Lecacheur, shouting with all my might:

"'Hullo, there! Mrs. Landlady, come here and look at this.'

"The rustic approached and looked at my work with her stupid eyes which distinguished nothing and could not even tell whether the picture represented an ox or a house.

"Miss Harriet just then came home, and she passed behind me just as I was holding out my canvas at arm's length, exhibiting it to our landlady. The demoniac could not help but see it, for I took care to exhibit the thing in such a way that it could not escape her notice. She stopped abruptly and stood motionless, astonished. It was her rock which was depicted, the one which she climbed to dream away her time undisturbed.

"She uttered a British 'Aoh,' which was at once so accentuated and so flattering that I turned round to her, smiling, and said:

"'This is my latest study, mademoiselle.'

"She murmured rapturously, comically and tenderly:

"'Oh! monsieur, you understand nature as a living thing.'

"I colored and was more touched by that compliment than if it had come from a queen. I was captured, conquered, vanquished. I could have embraced her, upon my honor.

"I took my seat at table beside her as usual. For the first time she spoke, thinking aloud:

"'Oh! I do love nature.'

"I passed her some bread, some water, some wine. She now accepted these with a little smile of a mummy. I then began to talk about the scenery.

"After the meal we rose from the table together and walked leisurely across the courtyard; then, attracted doubtless by the fiery glow which the setting sun cast over the surface of the sea, I opened the gate which led to the cliff, and we walked along side by side, as contented as two persons might be who have just learned to understand and penetrate each other's motives and feelings.

"It was one of those warm, soft evenings which impart a sense of ease to flesh and spirit alike. All is enjoyment, everything charms. The balmy air, laden with the perfume of grasses and the smell of seaweed, soothes the olfactory sense with its wild fragrance, soothes the palate with its sea savor, soothes the mind with its pervading sweetness.

"We were now walking along the edge of the cliff, high above the boundless sea which rolled its little waves below us at a distance of a hundred metres. And we drank in with open mouth and expanded chest that fresh breeze, briny from kissing the waves, that came from the ocean and passed across our faces.

"Wrapped in her plaid shawl, with a look of inspiration as she faced the breeze, the English woman gazed fixedly at the great sun ball as it descended toward the horizon. Far off in the distance a three-master in full sail was outlined on the blood-red sky and a steamship, somewhat nearer, passed along, leaving behind it a trail of smoke on the horizon. The red sun globe sank slowly lower and lower and presently touched the water just behind the motionless vessel, which, in its dazzling effulgence, looked as though framed in a flame of fire. We saw it plunge, grow smaller and disappear, swallowed up by the ocean.

"Miss Harriet gazed in rapture at the last gleams of the dying day. She seemed longing to embrace the sky, the sea, the whole landscape.

"She murmured: 'Aoh! I love--I love' I saw a tear in her eye. She continued: 'I wish I were a little bird, so that I could mount up into the firmament.'

"She remained standing as I had often before seen her, perched on the cliff, her face as red as her shawl. I should have liked to have sketched her in my album. It would have been a caricature of ecstasy.

"I turned away so as not to laugh.

"I then spoke to her of painting as I would have done to a fellow artist, using the technical terms common among the devotees of the profession. She listened attentively, eagerly seeking to divine the meaning of the terms, so as to understand my thoughts. From time to time she would exclaim:

"'Oh! I understand, I understand. It is very interesting.'

"We returned home.

53

"The next day, on seeing me, she approached me, cordially holding out her hand; and we at once became firm friends.

"She was a good creature who had a kind of soul on springs, which became enthusiastic at a bound. She lacked equilibrium like all women who are spinsters at the age of fifty. She seemed to be preserved in a pickle of innocence, but her heart still retained something very youthful and inflammable. She loved both nature and animals with a fervor, a love like old wine fermented through age, with a sensuous love that she had never bestowed on men.

"One thing is certain, that the sight of a bitch nursing her puppies, a mare roaming in a meadow with a foal at its side, a bird's nest full of young ones, screaming, with their open mouths and their enormous heads, affected her perceptibly.

"Poor, solitary, sad, wandering beings! I love you ever since I became acquainted with Miss Harriet.

"I soon discovered that she had something she would like to tell me, but dare not, and I was amused at her timidity. When I started out in the morning with my knapsack on my back, she would accompany me in silence as far as the end of the village, evidently struggling to find words with which to begin a conversation. Then she would leave me abruptly and walk away quickly with her springy step.

"One day, however, she plucked up courage:

"I would like to see how you paint pictures. Are you willing? I have been very curious.'

"And she blushed as if she had said something very audacious.

"I conducted her to the bottom of the Petit-Val, where I had begun a large picture.

"She remained standing behind me, following all my gestures with concentrated attention. Then, suddenly, fearing perhaps that she was disturbing me, she said: 'Thank you,' and walked away.

"But she soon became more friendly, and accompanied me every day, her countenance exhibiting visible pleasure. She carried her camp stool under her arm, not permitting me to carry it. She would remain there for hours, silent and motionless, following with her eyes the point of my brush, in its every movement. When I obtained unexpectedly just the effect I wanted by a dash of color put on with the palette knife, she involuntarily uttered a little 'Ah!' of astonishment, of joy, of admiration. She had the most tender respect for my canvases, an almost religious respect for that human reproduction of a part of nature's work divine. My studies appeared to her a kind of religious pictures, and sometimes she spoke to me of God, with the idea of converting me.

"Oh, he was a queer, good-natured being, this God of hers! He was a sort of village philosopher without any great resources and without great power, for she always figured him to herself as inconsolable over injustices committed under his eyes, as though he were powerless to prevent them.

"She was, however, on excellent terms with him, affecting even to be the confidante of his secrets and of his troubles. She would say:

"'God wills' or 'God does not will,' just like a sergeant announcing to a recruit: 'The colonel has commanded.'

"At the bottom of her heart she deplored my ignorance of the intentions of the Eternal, which she endeavored to impart to me.

"Almost every day I found in my pockets, in my hat when I lifted it from the ground, in my paintbox, in my polished shoes, standing in front of my door in the morning, those little pious tracts which she no doubt, received directly from Paradise.

"I treated her as one would an old friend, with unaffected cordiality. But I soon perceived that she had changed somewhat in her manner, though, for a while, I paid little attention to it.

"When I was painting, whether in my valley or in some country lane, I would see her suddenly appear with her rapid, springy walk. She would then sit down abruptly, out of breath, as though she had been running or were overcome by some profound emotion. Her face would be red, that English red which is denied to the people of all other countries; then, without any reason, she would turn ashy pale and seem about to faint away. Gradually, however, her natural color would return and she would begin to speak.

"Then, without warning, she would break off in the middle of a sentence, spring up from her seat and walk away so rapidly and so strangely that I was at my wits' ends to discover whether I had done or said anything to displease or wound her.

"I finally came to the conclusion that those were her normal manners, somewhat modified no doubt in my honor during the first days of our acquaintance.

"When she returned to the farm, after walking for hours on the windy coast, her long curls often hung straight down, as if their springs had been broken. This had hitherto seldom given her any concern, and she would come to dinner without embarrassment all dishevelled by her sister, the breeze.

"But now she would go to her room and arrange the untidy locks, and when I would say, with familiar gallantry, which, however, always offended her:

"'You are as beautiful as a star to-day, Miss Harriet,' a blush would immediately rise to her cheeks, the blush of a young girl, of a girl of fifteen.

"Then she would suddenly become quite reserved and cease coming to watch me paint. I thought, 'This is only a fit of temper; it will blow over.' But it did not always blow over, and when I spoke to her she would answer me either with affected indifference or with sullen annoyance.

"She became by turns rude, impatient and nervous. I never saw her now except at meals, and we spoke but little. I concluded at length that I must have offended her in some way, and, accordingly, I said to her one evening:

"'Miss Harriet, why is it that you do not act toward me as formerly? What have I done to displease you? You are causing me much pain!'

"She replied in a most comical tone of anger:

"'I am just the same with you as formerly. It is not true, not true,' and she ran upstairs and shut herself up in her room.

"Occasionally she would look at me in a peculiar manner. I have often said to myself since then that those who are condemned to death must look thus when they are informed that their last day has come. In her eye there lurked a species of insanity, an insanity at once mystical and violent; and even more, a fever, an aggravated longing, impatient and impotent, for the unattained and unattainable.

"Nay, it seemed to me there was also going on within her a struggle in which her heart wrestled with an unknown force that she sought to master, and even, perhaps, something else. But what do I know? What do I know?

"It was indeed a singular revelation.

"For some time I had commenced to work, as soon as daylight appeared, on a picture the subject of which was as follows:

"A deep ravine, enclosed, surmounted by two thickets of trees and vines, extended into the distance and was lost, submerged in that milky vapor, in that cloud like cotton down that sometimes floats over valleys at daybreak. And at the extreme end of that heavy, transparent fog one saw, or, rather, surmised, that a couple of human beings were approaching, a human couple, a youth and a maiden, their arms interlaced, embracing each other, their heads inclined toward each other, their lips meeting.

"A first ray of the sun, glistening through the branches, pierced that fog of the dawn, illuminated it with a rosy reflection just behind the rustic lovers, framing their vague shadows in a silvery background. It was well done; yes, indeed, well done.

"I was working on the declivity which led to the Valley of Etretat. On this particular morning I had, by chance, the sort of floating vapor which I needed. Suddenly something rose up in front of me like a phantom; it was Miss Harriet. On seeing me she was about to flee. But I called after her, saying: 'Come here, come here, mademoiselle. I have a nice little picture for you.'

"She came forward, though with seeming reluctance. I handed her my sketch. She said nothing, but stood for a long time, motionless, looking at it, and suddenly she burst into tears. She wept spasmodically, like men who have striven hard to restrain their tears, but who can do so no longer and abandon themselves to grief, though still resisting. I sprang to my feet, moved at the sight of a sorrow I did not comprehend, and I took her by the hand with an impulse of brusque affection, a true French impulse which acts before it reflects.

"She let her hands rest in mine for a few seconds, and I felt them quiver as if all her nerves were being wrenched. Then she withdrew her hands abruptly, or, rather, snatched them away.

"I recognized that tremor, for I had felt it, and I could not be deceived. Ah! the love tremor of a woman, whether she be fifteen or fifty years of age, whether she be of the people or of society, goes so straight to my heart that I never have any hesitation in understanding it!

"Her whole frail being had trembled, vibrated, been overcome. I knew it. She walked away before I had time to say a word, leaving me as surprised as if I had witnessed a miracle and as troubled as if I had committed a crime.

"I did not go in to breakfast. I went to take a turn on the edge of the cliff, feeling that I would just as lief weep as laugh, looking on the adventure as both comic and deplorable and my position as ridiculous, believing her unhappy enough to go insane.

"I asked myself what I ought to do. It seemed best for me to leave the place, and I immediately resolved to do so.

"Somewhat sad and perplexed, I wandered about until dinner time and entered the farmhouse just when the soup had been served up.

"I sat down at the table as usual. Miss Harriet was there, eating away solemnly, without speaking to any one, without even lifting her eyes. Her manner and expression were, however, the same as usual.

"I waited patiently till the meal had been finished, when, turning toward the landlady, I said: 'Well, Madame Lecacheur, it will not be long now before I shall have to take my leave of you.'

"The good woman, at once surprised and troubled, replied in her drawling voice: 'My dear sir, what is it you say? You are going to leave us after I have become so accustomed to you?'

"I glanced at Miss Harriet out of the corner of my eye. Her countenance did not change in the least. But Celeste, the little servant, looked up at me. She was a fat girl, of about eighteen years of age, rosy, fresh, as strong as a horse, and possessing the rare attribute of cleanliness. I had kissed her at odd times in out-of-the-way corners, after the manner of travellers--nothing more.

"The dinner being at length over, I went to smoke my pipe under the apple trees, walking up and down from one end of the enclosure to the other. All the reflections which I had made during the day, the strange discovery of the morning, that passionate and grotesque attachment for me, the recollections which that revelation had suddenly called up, recollections at once charming and perplexing, perhaps also that look which the servant had cast on me at the announcement of my departure--all these things, mixed up and combined, put me now in a reckless humor, gave me a tickling sensation of kisses on the lips and in my veins a something which urged me on to commit some folly.

"Night was coming on, casting its dark shadows under the trees, when I descried Celeste, who had gone to fasten up the poultry yard at the other end of the enclosure. I darted toward her, running so noiselessly that she heard nothing, and as she got up from closing the small trapdoor by which the chickens got in and out, I clasped her in my arms and rained on her coarse, fat face a shower of kisses. She struggled, laughing all the time, as she was accustomed to do in such circumstances. Why did I suddenly loose my grip of her? Why did I at once experience a shock? What was it that I heard behind me?

"It was Miss Harriet, who had come upon us, who had seen us and who stood in front of us motionless as a spectre. Then she disappeared in the darkness.

"I was ashamed, embarrassed, more desperate at having been thus surprised by her than if she had caught me committing some criminal act.

"I slept badly that night. I was completely unnerved and haunted by sad thoughts. I seemed to hear loud weeping, but in this I was no doubt deceived. Moreover, I thought several times that I heard some one walking up and down in the house and opening the hall door.

"Toward morning I was overcome by fatigue and fell asleep. I got up late and did not go downstairs until the late breakfast, being still in a bewildered state, not knowing what kind of expression to put on.

"No one had seen Miss Harriet. We waited for her at table, but she did not appear. At length Mother Lecacheur went to her room. The English woman had gone out. She must have set out at break of day, as she was wont to do, in order to see the sun rise.

"Nobody seemed surprised at this, and we began to eat in silence.

"The weather was hot, very hot, one of those broiling, heavy days when not a leaf stirs. The table had been placed out of doors, under an apple tree, and from time to time Sapeur had gone to the cellar to draw a jug of cider, everybody was so thirsty. Celeste brought the dishes from the kitchen, a ragout of mutton with potatoes, a cold rabbit and a salad. Afterward she placed before us a dish of strawberries, the first of the season.

"As I wished to wash and freshen these, I begged the servant to go and draw me a pitcher of cold water.

"In about five minutes she returned, declaring that the well was dry. She had lowered the pitcher to the full extent of the cord and had touched the bottom, but on drawing the pitcher up again it was empty. Mother Lecacheur, anxious to examine the thing for herself, went and looked down the hole. She returned, announcing that one could see clearly something in the well, something altogether unusual. But this no doubt was bundles of straw, which a neighbor had thrown in out of spite.

"I wished to look down the well also, hoping I might be able to clear up the mystery, and I perched myself close to the brink. I perceived indistinctly a white object. What could it be? I then conceived the idea of lowering a lantern at the end of a cord. When I did so the yellow flame danced on the layers of stone and gradually became clearer. All four of us were leaning over the opening, Sapeur and Celeste having now joined us. The lantern rested on a black-and-white indistinct mass, singular, incomprehensible. Sapeur exclaimed:

"'It is a horse. I see the hoofs. It must have got out of the meadow during the night and fallen in headlong.'

"But suddenly a cold shiver froze me to the marrow. I first recognized a foot, then a leg sticking up; the whole body and the other leg were completely under water.

"I stammered out in a loud voice, trembling so violently that the lantern danced hither and thither over the slipper:

"'It is a woman! Who-who-can it be? It is Miss Harriet!'

"Sapeur alone did not manifest horror. He had witnessed many such scenes in Africa.

"Mother Lecacheur and Celeste began to utter piercing screams and ran away.

"But it was necessary to recover the corpse of the dead woman. I attached the young man securely by the waist to the end of the pulley rope and lowered him very slowly, watching him disappear in the darkness. In one hand he held the lantern and a rope in the other. Soon I recognized his voice, which seemed to come from the centre of the earth, saying:

"'Stop!'

"I then saw him fish something out of the water. It was the other leg. He then bound the two feet together and shouted anew:

"'Haul up!'

"I began to wind up, but I felt my arms crack, my muscles twitch, and I was in terror lest I should let the man fall to the bottom. When his head appeared at the brink I asked:

"'Well?' as if I expected he had a message from the drowned woman.

"We both got on the stone slab at the edge of the well and from opposite sides we began to haul up the body.

"Mother Lecacheur and Celeste watched us from a distance, concealed from view behind the wall of the house. When they saw issuing from the hole the black slippers and white stockings of the drowned person they disappeared.

"Sapeur seized the ankles, and we drew up the body of the poor woman. The head was shocking to look at, being bruised and lacerated, and the long gray hair, out of curl forevermore, hanging down tangled and disordered.

61

"'In the name of all that is holy! how lean she is,' exclaimed Sapeur in a contemptuous tone.

"We carried her into the room, and as the women did not put in an appearance I, with the assistance of the stable lad, dressed the corpse for burial.

"I washed her disfigured face. Under the touch of my finger an eye was slightly opened and regarded me with that pale, cold look, that terrible look of a corpse which seems to come from the beyond. I braided as well as I could her dishevelled hair and with my clumsy hands arranged on her head a novel and singular coiffure. Then I took off her dripping wet garments, baring, not without a feeling of shame, as though I had been guilty of some profanation, her shoulders and her chest and her long arms, as slim as the twigs of a tree.

"I next went to fetch some flowers, poppies, bluets, marguerites and fresh, sweet-smelling grass with which to strew her funeral couch.

"I then had to go through the usual formalities, as I was alone to attend to everything. A letter found in her pocket, written at the last moment, requested that her body be buried in the village in which she had passed the last days of her life. A sad suspicion weighed on my heart. Was it not on my account that she wished to be laid to rest in this place?

"Toward evening all the female gossips of the locality came to view the rémains of the defunct, but I would not allow a single person to enter. I wanted to be alone, and I watched beside her all night.

"I looked at the corpse by the flickering light of the candles, at this unhappy woman, unknown to us all, who had died in such a lamentable manner and so far away from home. Had she left no friends, no relations behind her? What had her infancy been? What had been her life? Whence had she come thither alone, a wanderer, lost like a dog driven from home? What secrets of sufferings and of despair were sealed up in that unprepossessing body, in that poor body whose outward appearance had driven from her all affection, all love?

"How many unhappy beings there are! I felt that there weighed upon that human creature the eternal injustice of implacable nature! It was all over with her, without her ever having experienced, perhaps, that which sustains the greatest outcasts to wit, the hope of being loved once! Otherwise why should she thus have concealed herself, fled from the face of others? Why did she love everything so tenderly and so passionately, everything living that was not a man?

"I recognized the fact that she believed in a God, and that she hoped to receive compensation from the latter for all the miseries she had endured. She would now disintegrate and become, in turn, a plant. She would blossom in the sun, the cattle would browse on her leaves, the birds would bear away the seeds, and through these changes she would become again human flesh. But that which is called the soul had been extinguished at the bottom of the dark well. She suffered no longer. She had given her life for that of others yet to come.

"Hours passed away in this silent and sinister communion with the dead. A pale light at length announced the dawn of a new day; then a red ray streamed in on the bed, making a bar of light across the coverlet and across her hands. This was the hour she had so much loved. The awakened birds began to sing in the trees.

"I opened the window to its fullest extent and drew back the curtains that the whole heavens might look in upon us, and, bending over the icy corpse, I took in my hands the mutilated head and slowly, without terror or disgust, I imprinted a kiss, a long kiss, upon those lips which had never before been kissed."

Leon Chenal remained silent. The women wept. We heard on the box seat the Count d'Atraille blowing his nose from time to time. The coachman alone had gone to sleep. The horses, who no longer felt the sting of the whip, had slackened their pace and moved along slowly. The drag, hardly advancing at all, seemed suddenly torpid, as if it had been freighted with sorrow.

[Miss Harriet appeared in Le Gaulois, July 9, 1883, under the title of Miss Hastings. The story was later revised, enlarged; and partly reconstructed. This is what De Maupassant wrote to Editor Havard March 15, 1884, in an unedited letter, in regard to the title of the story that was to give its name to the volume:

"I do not believe that Hastings is a bad name, inasmuch as it is known all over the world, and recalls the greatest facts in English history. Besides, Hastings is as much a name as Duval is with us.

"The name Cherbuliez selected, Miss Revel, is no more like an English name than like a Turkish name. But here is another name as English as Hastings, and more euphonious; it is Miss Harriet. I will ask you therefore to substitute Harriet for Hastings."

It was in regard to this very tittle that De Maupassant had a disagreement with Audran and Boucheron director of the Bouffes Parisiens in October, 1890 They had given this title to an operetta about to be played at the Bouffes. It ended however, by their ceding to De Maupassant, and the title of the operetta was changed to Miss Helyett.]

BOULE DE SUIF

For several days in succession fragments of a defeated army had passed through the town. They were mere disorganized bands, not disciplined forces. The men wore long, dirty beards and tattered uniforms; they advanced in listless fashion, without a flag, without a leader. All seemed exhausted, worn out, incapable of thought or resolve, marching onward merely by force of habit, and dropping to the ground with fatigue the moment they halted. One saw, in particular, many enlisted men, peaceful citizens, men who lived quietly on their income, bending beneath the weight of their rifles; and little active volunteers, easily frightened but full of enthusiasm, as eager to attack as they were ready to take to flight; and amid these, a sprinkling of red-breeched soldiers, the pitiful remnant of a division cut down in a great battle; somber artillerymen, side by side with nondescript foot-soldiers; and, here and there, the gleaming helmet of a heavy-footed dragoon who had difficulty in keeping up with the quicker pace of the soldiers of the line. Legions of irregulars with high-sounding names "Avengers of Defeat," "Citizens of the Tomb," "Brethren in Death"--passed in their turn, looking like banditti. Their leaders, former drapers or grain merchants, or tallow or soap chandlers--warriors by force of circumstances, officers by reason of their mustachios or their money--covered with weapons, flannel and gold lace, spoke in an impressive manner, discussed plans of campaign, and behaved as though they alone bore the fortunes of dying France on their braggart shoulders; though, in truth, they frequently were afraid of their own men--scoundrels often brave beyond measure, but pillagers and debauchees.

Rumor had it that the Prussians were about to enter Rouen.

The members of the National Guard, who for the past two months had been reconnoitering with the utmost caution in the neighboring woods, occasionally shooting their own sentinels, and making ready for fight whenever a rabbit rustled in the undergrowth, had now returned to their homes. Their arms, their uniforms, all the death-dealing paraphernalia with which they had terrified all the milestones along the highroad for eight miles round, had suddenly and marvellously disappeared.

The last of the French soldiers had just crossed the Seine on their way to Pont-Audemer, through Saint-Sever and Bourg-Achard, and in their rear the vanquished general, powerless to do aught with the forlorn remnants of his army, himself dismayed at the final overthrow of a nation accustomed to victory and disastrously beaten despite its legendary bravery, walked between two orderlies.

Then a profound calm, a shuddering, silent dread, settled on the city. Many a round-paunched citizen, emasculated by years devoted to business, anxiously awaited the conquerors, trembling lest his roasting-jacks or kitchen knives should be looked upon as weapons.

Life seemed to have stopped short; the shops were shut, the streets deserted. Now and then an inhabitant, awed by the silence, glided swiftly by in the shadow of the walls. The anguish of suspense made men even desire the arrival of the enemy.

In the afternoon of the day following the departure of the French troops, a number of uhlans, coming no one knew whence, passed rapidly through the town. A little later on, a black mass descended St. Catherine's Hill, while two other invading bodies appeared respectively on the Darnetal and the Boisguillaume roads. The advance guards of the three corps arrived at precisely the same moment at the Square of the Hotel de Ville, and the German army poured through all the adjacent streets, its battalions making the pavement ring with their firm, measured tread.

Orders shouted in an unknown, guttural tongue rose to the windows of the seemingly dead, deserted houses; while behind the fast-closed shutters eager eyes peered forth at the victors-masters now of the city, its fortunes, and its lives, by "right of war." The inhabitants, in their darkened rooms, were possessed by that terror which follows in the wake of cataclysms, of deadly upheavals of the earth, against which all human skill and strength are vain. For the same thing happens whenever the established order of things is upset, when security no longer exists, when all those rights usually protected by the law of man or of Nature are at the mercy of unreasoning, savage force. The earthquake crushing a whole nation under falling roofs; the flood let loose, and engulfing in its swirling depths the corpses of drowned peasants, along with dead oxen and beams torn from shattered houses; or the army, covered with glory, murdering those who defend themselves, making prisoners of the rest, pillaging in the name of the Sword, and giving thanks to God to the thunder of cannon--all these are appalling scourges, which destroy all belief in eternal

66

justice, all that confidence we have been taught to feel in the protection of Heaven and the reason of man.

Small detachments of soldiers knocked at each door, and then disappeared within the houses; for the vanquished saw they would have to be civil to their conquerors.

At the end of a short time, once the first terror had subsided, calm was again restored. In many houses the Prussian officer ate at the same table with the family. He was often well-bred, and, out of politeness, expressed sympathy with France and repugnance at being compelled to take part in the war. This sentiment was received with gratitude; besides, his protection might be needful some day or other. By the exercise of tact the number of men quartered in one's house might be reduced; and why should one provoke the hostility of a person on whom one's whole welfare depended? Such conduct would savor less of bravery than of fool- hardiness. And foolhardiness is no longer a failing of the citizens of Rouen as it was in the days when their city earned renown by its heroic defenses. Last of all-final argument based on the national politeness- the folk of Rouen said to one another that it was only right to be civil in one's own house, provided there was no public exhibition of familiarity with the foreigner. Out of doors, therefore, citizen and soldier did not know each other; but in the house both chatted freely, and each evening the German remained a little longer warming himself at the hospitable hearth.

Even the town itself resumed by degrees its ordinary aspect. The French seldom walked abroad, but the streets swarmed with Prussian soldiers. Moreover, the officers of the Blue Hussars, who arrogantly dragged their instruments of death along the pavements, seemed to hold the simple townsmen in but little more contempt than did the French cavalry officers who had drunk at the same cafes the year before.

But there was something in the air, a something strange and subtle, an intolerable foreign atmosphere like a penetrating odor--the odor of invasion. It permeated dwellings and places of public resort, changed the taste of food, made one imagine one's self in far-distant lands, amid dangerous, barbaric tribes.

The conquerors exacted money, much money. The inhabitants paid what was asked; they were rich. But, the wealthier a Norman tradesman becomes, the more he suffers at having to part with anything that belongs to him, at having to see any portion of his substance pass into the hands of another.

Nevertheless, within six or seven miles of the town, along the course of the river as it flows onward to Croisset, Dieppedalle and Biessart, boat- men and fishermen often hauled to the surface of the water the body of a German, bloated in his uniform, killed by a blow from knife or club, his head crushed by a stone, or perchance pushed from some bridge into the stream below. The mud of the river-bed swallowed up these obscure acts of vengeance--savage, yet legitimate; these unrecorded deeds of bravery; these silent attacks fraught with greater danger than battles fought in broad day, and surrounded, moreover, with no halo of romance. For hatred of the foreigner ever arms a few intrepid souls, ready to die for an idea.

At last, as the invaders, though subjecting the town to the strictest discipline, had not committed any of the deeds of horror with which they had been credited while on their triumphal march, the people grew bolder, and the necessities of business again animated the breasts of the local merchants. Some of these had important commercial interests at Havre- occupied at present by the French army--and wished to attempt to reach that port by overland route to Dieppe, taking the boat from there.

Through the influence of the German officers whose acquaintance they had made, they obtained a permit to leave town from the general in command.

A large four-horse coach having, therefore, been engaged for the journey, and ten passengers having given in their names to the proprietor, they decided to start on a certain Tuesday morning before daybreak, to avoid attracting a crowd.

The ground had been frozen hard for some time-past, and about three o'clock on Monday afternoon--large black clouds from the north shed their burden of snow uninterruptedly all through that evening and night.

At half-past four in the morning the travellers met in the courtyard of the Hotel de Normandie, where they were to take their seats in the coach.

They were still half asleep, and shivering with cold under their wraps. They could see one another but indistinctly in the darkness, and the mountain of heavy winter wraps in which each was swathed made them look like a gathering of obese priests in their long cassocks. But two men recognized each other, a third accosted them, and the three began to talk. "I am bringing my wife," said one. "So am I." "And I, too." The first speaker added: "We shall not return to Rouen, and if the Prussians approach Havre we will cross to

England." All three, it turned out, had made the same plans, being of similar disposition and temperament.

Still the horses were not harnessed. A small lantern carried by a stable-boy emerged now and then from one dark doorway to disappear immediately in another. The stamping of horses' hoofs, deadened by the dung and straw of the stable, was heard from time to time, and from inside the building issued a man's voice, talking to the animals and swearing at them. A faint tinkle of bells showed that the harness was being got ready; this tinkle soon developed into a continuous jingling, louder or softer according to the movements of the horse, sometimes stopping altogether, then breaking out in a sudden peal accompanied by a pawing of the ground by an iron-shod hoof.

The door suddenly closed. All noise ceased.

The frozen townsmen were silent; they remained motionless, stiff with cold.

A thick curtain of glistening white flakes fell ceaselessly to the ground; it obliterated all outlines, enveloped all objects in an icy mantle of foam; nothing was to be heard throughout the length and breadth of the silent, winter-bound city save the vague, nameless rustle of falling snow--a sensation rather than a sound--the gentle mingling of light atoms which seemed to fill all space, to cover the whole world.

The man reappeared with his lantern, leading by a rope a melancholy- looking horse, evidently being led out against his inclination. The hostler placed him beside the pole, fastened the traces, and spent some time in walking round him to make sure that the harness was all right; for he could use only one hand, the other being engaged in holding the lantern. As he was about to fetch the second horse he noticed the motionless group of travellers, already white with snow, and said to them: "Why don't you get inside the coach? You'd be under shelter, at least."

This did not seem to have occurred to them, and they at once took his advice. The three men seated their wives at the far end of the coach, then got in themselves; lastly the other vague, snow-shrouded forms clambered to the remaining places without a word.

The floor was covered with straw, into which the feet sank. The ladies at the far end, having brought with them little copper foot-warmers heated by means of a kind of chemical fuel, proceeded to light these, and spent some time in expatiating in low tones on their advantages, saying over and over again things which they had all known for a long time.

At last, six horses instead of four having been harnessed to the diligence, on account of the heavy roads, a voice outside asked: "Is every one there?" To which a voice from the interior replied: "Yes," and they set out.

The vehicle moved slowly, slowly, at a snail's pace; the wheels sank into the snow; the entire body of the coach creaked and groaned; the horses slipped, puffed, steamed, and the coachman's long whip cracked incessantly, flying hither and thither, coiling up, then flinging out its length like a slender serpent, as it lashed some rounded flank, which instantly grew tense as it strained in further effort.

But the day grew apace. Those light flakes which one traveller, a native of Rouen, had compared to a rain of cotton fell no longer. A murky light filtered through dark, heavy clouds, which made the country more dazzlingly white by contrast, a whiteness broken sometimes by a row of tall trees spangled with hoarfrost, or by a cottage roof hooded in snow.

Within the coach the passengers eyed one another curiously in the dim light of dawn.

Right at the back, in the best seats of all, Monsieur and Madame Loiseau, wholesale wine merchants of the Rue Grand-Pont, slumbered opposite each other. Formerly clerk to a merchant who had failed in business, Loiseau had bought his master's interest, and made a fortune for himself. He sold very bad wine at a very low price to the retail-dealers in the country, and had the reputation, among his friends and acquaintances, of being a shrewd rascal a true Norman, full of quips and wiles. So well established was his character as a cheat that, in the mouths of the citizens of Rouen, the very name of Loiseau became a byword for sharp practice.

Above and beyond this, Loiseau was noted for his practical jokes of every description--his tricks, good or ill-natured; and no one could mention his name without adding at once: "He's an extraordinary man--Loiseau." He was undersized and potbellied, had a florid face with grayish whiskers.

His wife-tall, strong, determined, with a loud voice and decided manner--represented the spirit of order and arithmetic in the business house which Loiseau enlivened by his jovial activity.

Beside them, dignified in bearing, belonging to a superior caste, sat Monsieur Carre-Lamadon, a man of considerable importance, a king in the cotton trade, proprietor of three spinning-mills, officer of the Legion of Honor, and member of the General Council. During the whole time the Empire was in the ascendancy he remained the chief of the well-disposed Opposition, merely in order to command a higher value for his devotion when he should rally to the cause which he meanwhile opposed with "courteous weapons," to use his own expression.

Madame Carre-Lamadon, much younger than her husband, was the consolation of all the officers of good family quartered at Rouen. Pretty, slender, graceful, she sat opposite her husband, curled up in her furs, and gazing mournfully at the sorry interior of the coach.

Her neighbors, the Comte and Comtesse Hubert de Breville, bore one of the noblest and most ancient names in Normandy. The count, a nobleman advanced in years and of aristocratic bearing, strove to enhance by every artifice of the toilet, his natural resemblance to King Henry IV, who, according to a legend of which the family were inordinately proud, had been the favored lover of a De Breville lady, and father of her child-- the frail one's husband having, in recognition of this fact, been made a count and governor of a province.

A colleague of Monsieur Carre-Lamadon in the General Council, Count Hubert represented the Orleanist party in his department. The story of his marriage with the daughter of a small shipowner at Nantes had always remained more or less of a mystery. But as the countess had an air of unmistakable breeding, entertained faultlessly, and was even supposed to have been loved by a son of Louis-Philippe, the nobility vied with one another in doing her honor, and her drawing-room remained the most select in the whole countryside--the only one which retained the old spirit of gallantry, and to which access was not easy.

The fortune of the Brevilles, all in real estate, amounted, it was said, to five hundred thousand francs a year.

These six people occupied the farther end of the coach, and represented Society--with an income--the strong, established society of good people with religion and principle.

It happened by chance that all the women were seated on the same side; and the countess had, moreover, as neighbors two nuns, who spent the time in fingering their long rosaries and murmuring paternosters and aves. One of them was old, and so deeply pitted with smallpox that she looked for all the world as if she had received a charge of shot full in the face. The other, of sickly appearance, had a pretty but wasted countenance, and a narrow, consumptive chest, sapped by that devouring faith which is the making of martyrs and visionaries.

A man and woman, sitting opposite the two nuns, attracted all eyes.

The man--a well-known character--was Cornudet, the democrat, the terror of all respectable people. For the past twenty years his big red beard had been on terms of intimate acquaintance with the tankards of all the republican cafes. With the help of his comrades and brethren he had dissipated a respectable fortune left him by his father, an old- established confectioner, and he now impatiently awaited the Republic, that he might at last be rewarded with the post he had earned by his revolutionary orgies. On the fourth of September-- possibly as the result of a practical joke--he was led to believe that he had been appointed prefect; but when he attempted to take up the duties of the position the clerks in charge of the office refused to recognize his authority, and he was compelled in consequence to retire. A good sort of fellow in other respects, inoffensive and obliging, he had thrown himself zealously into the work of making an organized defence of the town. He had had pits dug in the level country, young forest trees felled, and traps set on all the roads; then at the approach of the enemy, thoroughly satisfied with his preparations, he had hastily returned to the town. He thought he might now do more good at Havre, where new intrenchments would soon be necessary.

The woman, who belonged to the courtesan class, was celebrated for an embonpoint unusual for her age, which had earned for her the sobriquet of "Boule de Suif" (Tallow Ball). Short and round, fat as a pig, with puffy fingers constricted at the joints, looking like rows of short sausages; with a shiny, tightly-stretched skin and an enormous bust filling out the bodice of her dress, she was yet attractive and much sought after, owing to her fresh and pleasing appearance. Her face was like a crimson apple, a peony-bud just bursting into bloom; she had two magnificent dark eyes, fringed with thick, heavy lashes, which cast a shadow into their depths; her mouth was small, ripe, kissable, and was furnished with the tiniest of white teeth.

As soon as she was recognized the respectable matrons of the party began to whisper among themselves, and the words "hussy" and "public scandal" were uttered so loudly that Boule de Suif raised her head. She forthwith cast such a challenging, bold look at her neighbors that a sudden silence fell on the company, and all lowered their eyes, with the exception of Loiseau, who watched her with evident interest.

But conversation was soon resumed among the three ladies, whom the presence of this girl had suddenly drawn together in the bonds of friendship-- one might almost say in those of intimacy. They decided that they ought to combine, as it were, in their dignity as wives in face of this shameless hussy; for legitimized love always despises its easygoing brother.

The three men, also, brought together by a certain conservative instinct awakened by the presence of Cornudet, spoke of money matters in a tone expressive of contempt for the poor. Count Hubert related the losses he had sustained at the hands of the Prussians, spoke of the cattle which had been stolen from him, the crops which had been ruined, with the easy manner of a nobleman who was also a tenfold millionaire, and whom such reverses would scarcely inconvenience for a single year. Monsieur Carre- Lamadon, a man of wide experience in the cotton industry, had taken care to send six hundred thousand francs to England as provision against the rainy day he was always anticipating. As for Loiseau, he had managed to sell to the French commissariat department all the wines he had in stock, so that the state now owed him a considerable sum, which he hoped to receive at Havre.

And all three eyed one another in friendly, well-disposed fashion. Although of varying social status, they were united in the brotherhood of money--in that vast freemasonry made up of those who possess, who can jingle gold wherever they choose to put their hands into their breeches' pockets.

The coach went along so slowly that at ten o'clock in the morning it had not covered twelve miles. Three times the men of the party got out and climbed the hills on foot. The passengers were becoming uneasy, for they had counted on lunching at Totes, and it seemed now as if they would hardly arrive there before nightfall. Every one was eagerly looking out for an inn by the roadside, when, suddenly, the coach foundered in a snowdrift, and it took two hours to extricate it.

As appetites increased, their spirits fell; no inn, no wine shop could be discovered, the approach of the Prussians and the transit of the starving French troops having frightened away all business.

The men sought food in the farmhouses beside the road, but could not find so much as a crust of bread; for the suspicious peasant invariably hid his stores for fear of being pillaged by the soldiers, who, being entirely without food, would take violent possession of everything they found.

About one o'clock Loiseau announced that he positively had a big hollow in his stomach. They had all been suffering in the same way for some time, and the increasing gnawings of hunger had put an end to all conversation.

Now and then some one yawned, another followed his example, and each in turn, according to his character, breeding and social position, yawned either quietly or noisily, placing his hand before the gaping void whence issued breath condensed into vapor.

Several times Boule de Suif stooped, as if searching for something under her petticoats. She would hesitate a moment, look at her neighbors, and then quietly sit upright again. All faces were pale and drawn. Loiseau declared he would give a thousand francs for a knuckle of ham. His wife made an involuntary and quickly checked gesture of protest. It always hurt her to hear of money being squandered, and she could not even understand jokes on such a subject.

"As a matter of fact, I don't feel well," said the count. "Why did I not think of bringing provisions?" Each one reproached himself in similar fashion.

Cornudet, however, had a bottle of rum, which he offered to his neighbors. They all coldly refused except Loiseau, who took a sip, and returned the bottle with thanks, saying: "That's good stuff; it warms one up, and cheats the appetite." The alcohol put him in good humor, and he proposed they should do as the sailors did in the song: eat the fattest of the passengers. This indirect allusion to Boule de Suif shocked the respectable members of the party. No one replied; only Cornudet smiled. The two good sisters had ceased to mumble their rosary, and, with hands enfolded in their wide sleeves, sat motionless, their eyes steadfastly cast down, doubtless offering up as a sacrifice to Heaven the suffering it had sent them.

At last, at three o'clock, as they were in the midst of an apparently limitless plain, with not a single village in sight, Boule de Suif stooped quickly, and drew from underneath the seat a large basket covered with a white napkin.

From this she extracted first of all a small earthenware plate and a silver drinking cup, then an enormous dish containing two whole chickens cut into joints and imbedded in jelly. The basket was seen to contain other good things: pies, fruit, dainties of all sorts-provisions, in fine, for a three days' journey, rendering their owner independent of wayside inns. The necks of four bottles protruded from among the food. She took a chicken wing, and began to eat it daintily, together with one of those rolls called in Normandy "Regence."

All looks were directed toward her. An odor of food filled the air, causing nostrils to dilate, mouths to water, and jaws to contract painfully. The scorn of the ladies for this disreputable female grew positively ferocious; they would have liked to kill her, or throw, her and her drinking cup, her basket, and her provisions, out of the coach into the snow of the road below.

But Loiseau's gaze was fixed greedily on the dish of chicken. He said:

"Well, well, this lady had more forethought than the rest of us. Some people think of everything."

She looked up at him.

"Would you like some, sir? It is hard to go on fasting all day."

He bowed.

"Upon my soul, I can't refuse; I cannot hold out another minute. All is fair in war time, is it not, madame?" And, casting a glance on those around, he added:

"At times like this it is very pleasant to meet with obliging people."

He spread a newspaper over his knees to avoid soiling his trousers, and, with a pocketknife he always carried, helped himself to a chicken leg coated with jelly, which he thereupon proceeded to devour.

Then Boule le Suif, in low, humble tones, invited the nuns to partake of her repast. They both accepted the offer unhesitatingly, and after a few stammered words of thanks began to eat quickly, without raising their eyes. Neither did Cornudet refuse his neighbor's offer, and, in combination with the nuns, a sort of table was formed by opening out the newspaper over the four pairs of knees.

Mouths kept opening and shutting, ferociously masticating and devouring the food. Loiseau, in his corner, was hard at work, and in low tones urged his wife to follow his example. She held out for a long time, but overstrained Nature gave way at last. Her husband, assuming his politest manner, asked their "charming companion" if he might be allowed to offer Madame Loiseau a small helping.

"Why, certainly, sir," she replied, with an amiable smile, holding out the dish.

When the first bottle of claret was opened some embarrassment was caused by the fact that there was only one drinking cup, but this was passed from one to another, after being wiped. Cornudet alone, doubtless in a spirit of gallantry, raised to his own lips that part of the rim which was still moist from those of his fair neighbor.

Then, surrounded by people who were eating, and well-nigh suffocated by the odor of food, the Comte and Comtesse de Breville and Monsieur and Madame Carre-Lamadon endured that hateful form of torture which has perpetuated the name of Tantalus. All at once the manufacturer's young wife heaved a sigh which made every one turn and look at her; she was white as the snow without; her eyes closed, her head fell forward; she had fainted. Her husband, beside himself, implored the help of his neighbors. No one seemed to know what to do until the elder of the two nuns, raising the patient's head, placed Boule de Suif's drinking cup to her lips, and made her swallow a few drops of wine. The pretty invalid moved, opened her eyes, smiled, and declared in a feeble voice that she was all right again. But, to prevent a recurrence of the catastrophe, the nun made her drink a cupful of claret, adding: "It's just hunger- that's what is wrong with you."

Then Boule de Suif, blushing and embarrassed, stammered, looking at the four passengers who were still fasting:

"'Mon Dieu', if I might offer these ladies and gentlemen----"

She stopped short, fearing a snub. But Loiseau continued:

"Hang it all, in such a case as this we are all brothers and sisters and ought to assist each other. Come, come, ladies, don't stand on ceremony, for goodness' sake! Do we even know whether we shall find a house in which to pass the night? At our present rate of going we sha'n't be at Totes till midday to-morrow."

They hesitated, no one daring to be the first to accept. But the count settled the question. He turned toward the abashed girl, and in his most distinguished manner said:

"We accept gratefully, madame."

As usual, it was only the first step that cost. This Rubicon once crossed, they set to work with a will. The basket was emptied. It still contained a pate de foie gras, a lark pie, a piece of smoked tongue, Crassane pears, Pont-Leveque gingerbread, fancy cakes, and a cup full of pickled gherkins and onions--Boule de Suif, like all women, being very fond of indigestible things.

They could not eat this girl's provisions without speaking to her. So they began to talk, stiffly at first; then, as she seemed by no means forward, with greater freedom. Mesdames de Breville and Carre-Lamadon, who were accomplished women of the world, were gracious and tactful. The countess especially displayed that amiable condescension characteristic of great ladies whom no contact with baser mortals can sully, and was absolutely charming. But the sturdy Madame Loiseau, who had the soul of a gendarme, continued morose, speaking little and eating much.

Conversation naturally turned on the war. Terrible stories were told about the Prussians, deeds of bravery were recounted of the French; and all these people who were fleeing themselves were ready to pay homage to the courage of their compatriots. Personal experiences soon followed, and Bottle le Suif related with genuine emotion, and with that warmth of language not uncommon in women of her class and temperament, how it came about that she had left Rouen.

"I thought at first that I should be able to stay," she said. "My house was well stocked with provisions, and it seemed better to put up with feeding a few soldiers than to banish myself goodness knows where. But when I saw these Prussians it was too much for me! My blood boiled with rage; I wept the whole day for very shame. Oh, if only I had been a man! I looked at them from my window--the fat swine, with their pointed helmets!--and my maid held my hands to keep me from throwing my furniture down on them. Then some of them were quartered on me; I flew at the throat of the first one who entered. They are just as easy to strangle as other men! And I'd have been the death of that one if I hadn't been dragged away from him by my hair. I had to hide after that. And as soon as I could get an opportunity I left the place, and here I am."

She was warmly congratulated. She rose in the estimation of her companions, who had not been so brave; and Cornudet listened to her with the approving and benevolent smile of an apostle, the smile a priest might wear in listening to a devotee praising God; for long-bearded democrats of his type have a monopoly of patriotism, just as priests have a monopoly of religion. He held forth in turn, with dogmatic self- assurance, in the style of the proclamations daily pasted on the walls of the town, winding up with a specimen of stump oratory in which he reviled "that besotted fool of a Louis-Napoleon."

But Boule de Suif was indignant, for she was an ardent Bonapartist. She turned as red as a cherry, and stammered in her wrath: "I'd just like to have seen you in his place--you and your sort! There would have been a nice mix-up. Oh, yes! It was you who betrayed that man. It would be impossible to live in France if we were governed by such rascals as you!"

Cornudet, unmoved by this tirade, still smiled a superior, contemptuous smile; and one felt that high words were impending, when the count interposed, and, not without difficulty, succeeded in calming the exasperated woman, saying that all sincere opinions ought to be respected. But the countess and the manufacturer's wife, imbued with the unreasoning hatred of the upper classes for the Republic, and instinct, moreover, with the affection felt by all women for the pomp and circumstance of despotic government, were drawn, in spite of themselves, toward this dignified young woman, whose opinions coincided so closely with their own.

The basket was empty. The ten people had finished its contents without difficulty amid general regret that it did not hold more. Conversation went on a little longer, though it flagged somewhat after the passengers had finished eating.

Night fell, the darkness grew deeper and deeper, and the cold made Boule de Suif shiver, in spite of her plumpness. So Madame de Breville offered her her foot-warmer, the fuel of which had been several times renewed since the morning, and she accepted the offer at once, for her feet were icy cold. Mesdames Carre-Lamadon and Loiseau gave theirs to the nuns.

The driver lighted his lanterns. They cast a bright gleam on a cloud of vapor which hovered over the sweating flanks of the horses, and on the roadside snow, which seemed to unroll as they went along in the changing light of the lamps.

All was now indistinguishable in the coach; but suddenly a movement occurred in the corner occupied by Boule de Suif and Cornudet; and Loiseau, peering into the gloom, fancied he saw the big, bearded democrat move hastily to one side, as if he had received a well-directed, though noiseless, blow in the dark.

Tiny lights glimmered ahead. It was Totes. The coach had been on the road eleven hours, which, with the three hours allotted the horses in four periods for feeding and breathing, made fourteen. It entered the town, and stopped before the Hotel du Commerce.

The coach door opened; a well-known noise made all the travellers start; it was the clanging of a scabbard, on the pavement; then a voice called out something in German.

Although the coach had come to a standstill, no one got out; it looked as if they were afraid of being murdered the moment they left their seats. Thereupon the driver appeared, holding in his hand one of his lanterns, which cast a sudden glow on the interior of the coach, lighting up the double row of startled faces, mouths agape, and eyes wide open in surprise and terror.

Beside the driver stood in the full light a German officer, a tall young man, fair and slender, tightly encased in his uniform like a woman in her corset, his flat shiny cap, tilted to one side of his head, making him look like an English hotel runner. His exaggerated mustache, long and straight and tapering to a point at either end in a single blond hair that could hardly be seen, seemed to weigh down the corners of his mouth and give a droop to his lips.

In Alsatian French he requested the travellers to alight, saying stiffly:

"Kindly get down, ladies and gentlemen."

The two nuns were the first to obey, manifesting the docility of holy women accustomed to submission on every occasion. Next appeared the count and countess, followed by the manufacturer and his wife, after whom came Loiseau, pushing his larger and better half before him.

"Good-day, sir," he said to the officer as he put his foot to the ground, acting on an impulse born of prudence rather than of politeness. The other, insolent like all in authority, merely stared without replying.

Boule de Suif and Cornudet, though near the door, were the last to alight, grave and dignified before the enemy. The stout girl tried to control herself and appear calm; the democrat stroked his long russet beard with a somewhat trembling hand. Both strove to maintain their dignity, knowing well that at such a time each individual is always looked upon as more or less typical of his nation; and, also, resenting the complaisant attitude of their companions, Boule de Suif tried to wear a bolder front than her neighbors, the virtuous women, while he, feeling that it was incumbent on him to set a good example, kept up the attitude of resistance which he had first assumed when he undertook to mine the high roads round Rouen.

They entered the spacious kitchen of the inn, and the German, having demanded the passports signed by the general in command, in which were mentioned the name, description and profession of each traveller, inspected them all minutely, comparing their appearance with the written particulars.

Then he said brusquely: "All right," and turned on his heel.

They breathed freely, All were still hungry; so supper was ordered. Half an hour was required for its preparation, and while two servants were apparently engaged in getting it ready the travellers went to look at their rooms. These all opened off a long corridor, at the end of which was a glazed door with a number on it.

They were just about to take their seats at table when the innkeeper appeared in person. He was a former horse dealer--a large, asthmatic individual, always wheezing, coughing, and clearing his throat. Follenvie was his patronymic.

He called:

"Mademoiselle Elisabeth Rousset?"

Boule de Suif started, and turned round.

"That is my name."

"Mademoiselle, the Prussian officer wishes to speak to you immediately."

"To me?"

"Yes; if you are Mademoiselle Elisabeth Rousset."

She hesitated, reflected a moment, and then declared roundly:

"That may be; but I'm not going."

They moved restlessly around her; every one wondered and speculated as to the cause of this order. The count approached:

"You are wrong, madame, for your refusal may bring trouble not only on yourself but also on all your companions. It never pays to resist those in authority. Your compliance with this request cannot possibly be fraught with any danger; it has probably been made because some formality or other was forgotten."

All added their voices to that of the count; Boule de Suif was begged, urged, lectured, and at last convinced; every one was afraid of the complications which might result from headstrong action on her part. She said finally:

"I am doing it for your sakes, remember that!"

The countess took her hand.

"And we are grateful to you."

She left the room. All waited for her return before commencing the meal. Each was distressed that he or she had not been sent for rather than this impulsive, quick-tempered girl, and each mentally rehearsed platitudes in case of being summoned also.

But at the end of ten minutes she reappeared breathing hard, crimson with indignation.

"Oh! the scoundrel! the scoundrel!" she stammered.

All were anxious to know what had happened; but she declined to enlighten them, and when the count pressed the point, she silenced him with much dignity, saying:

"No; the matter has nothing to do with you, and I cannot speak of it."

Then they took their places round a high soup tureen, from which issued an odor of cabbage. In spite of this coincidence, the supper was cheerful. The cider was good; the Loiseaus and the nuns drank it from motives of economy. The others ordered wine; Cornudet demanded beer. He had his own fashion of uncorking the bottle and making the beer foam, gazing at it as he inclined his glass and then raised it to a position between the lamp and his eye that he might judge of its color. When he drank, his great beard, which matched the color of his favorite beverage, seemed to tremble with affection; his eyes positively squinted in the endeavor not to lose sight of the beloved glass, and he looked for all the world as if he were fulfilling the only function for which he was born. He seemed to have established in his mind an affinity between the two great passions of his life--pale ale and revolution--and assuredly he could not taste the one without dreaming of the other.

Monsieur and Madame Follenvie dined at the end of the table. The man, wheezing like a broken-down locomotive, was too short-winded to talk when he was eating. But the wife was not silent a moment; she told how the Prussians had impressed her on their arrival, what they did, what they said; execrating them in the first place because they cost her money, and in the second because she had two sons in the army. She addressed herself principally to the countess, flattered at the opportunity of talking to a lady of quality.

Then she lowered her voice, and began to broach delicate subjects. Her husband interrupted her from time to time, saying:

"You would do well to hold your tongue, Madame Follenvie."

But she took no notice of him, and went on:

"Yes, madame, these Germans do nothing but eat potatoes and pork, and then pork and potatoes. And don't imagine for a moment that they are clean! No, indeed! And if only you saw them drilling for hours, indeed for days, together; they all collect in a field, then they do nothing but march backward and forward, and wheel this way and that. If only they would cultivate the land, or remain at home and work on their high roads! Really, madame, these soldiers are of no earthly use! Poor people have to feed and keep them, only in order that they may learn how to kill! True, I am only an old woman with no education, but when I see them wearing themselves out marching about from morning till night, I say to myself: When there are people who make discoveries that are of use to people, why should others take so much trouble to do harm? Really, now, isn't it a terrible thing to kill people, whether they are Prussians, or English, or Poles, or French? If we revenge ourselves on any one who injures us we do wrong, and are punished for it; but when our sons are shot down like partridges, that is all right, and decorations are given to the man who kills the most. No, indeed, I shall never be able to understand it."

Cornudet raised his voice:

"War is a barbarous proceeding when we attack a peaceful neighbor, but it is a sacred duty when undertaken in defence of one's country."

The old woman looked down:

"Yes; it's another matter when one acts in self-defence; but would it not be better to kill all the kings, seeing that they make war just to amuse themselves?"

Cornudet's eyes kindled.

"Bravo, citizens!" he said.

Monsieur Carre-Lamadon was reflecting profoundly. Although an ardent admirer of great generals, the peasant woman's sturdy common sense made him reflect on the wealth which might accrue to a country by the employment of so many idle hands now maintained at a great expense, of so much unproductive force, if they were employed in those great industrial enterprises which it will take centuries to complete.

But Loiseau, leaving his seat, went over to the innkeeper and began chatting in a low voice. The big man chuckled, coughed, sputtered; his enormous carcass shook with merriment at the pleasantries of the other; and he ended by buying six casks of claret from Loiseau to be delivered in spring, after the departure of the Prussians.

The moment supper was over every one went to bed, worn out with fatigue.

But Loiseau, who had been making his observations on the sly, sent his wife to bed, and amused himself by placing first his ear, and then his eye, to the bedroom keyhole, in order to discover what he called "the mysteries of the corridor."

At the end of about an hour he heard a rustling, peeped out quickly, and caught sight of Boule de Suif, looking more rotund than ever in a dressing-gown of blue cashmere trimmed with white lace. She held a candle in her hand, and directed her steps to the numbered door at the end of the corridor. But one of the side doors was partly opened, and when, at the end of a few minutes, she returned, Cornudet, in his shirt- sleeves, followed her. They spoke in low tones, then stopped short. Boule de Suif seemed to be stoutly denying him admission to her room. Unfortunately, Loiseau could not at first hear what they said; but toward the end of the conversation they raised their voices, and he caught a few words. Cornudet was loudly insistent.

"How silly you are! What does it matter to you?" he said.

She seemed indignant, and replied:

"No, my good man, there are times when one does not do that sort of thing; besides, in this place it would be shameful."

Apparently he did not understand, and asked the reason. Then she lost her temper and her caution, and, raising her voice still higher, said:

"Why? Can't you understand why? When there are Prussians in the house! Perhaps even in the very next room!"

He was silent. The patriotic shame of this wanton, who would not suffer herself to be caressed in the neighborhood of the enemy, must have roused his dormant dignity, for after bestowing on her a simple kiss he crept softly back to his room. Loiseau, much edified, capered round the bedroom before taking his place beside his slumbering spouse.

Then silence reigned throughout the house. But soon there arose from some remote part--it might easily have been either cellar or attic--a stertorous, monotonous, regular snoring, a dull, prolonged rumbling, varied by tremors like those of a boiler under pressure of steam. Monsieur Follenvie had gone to sleep.

As they had decided on starting at eight o'clock the next morning, every one was in the kitchen at that hour; but the coach, its roof covered with snow, stood by itself in the middle of the yard, without either horses or driver. They sought the latter in the stables, coach-houses and barns- but in vain. So the men of the party resolved to scour the country for him, and sallied forth. They found themselves in the square, with the church at the farther side, and to right and left low-roofed houses where there were some Prussian soldiers. The first soldier they saw was peeling potatoes. The second, farther on, was washing out a barber's shop. An other, bearded to the eyes, was fondling a crying infant, and dandling it on his knees to quiet it; and the stout peasant women, whose menfolk were for the most part at the war, were, by means of signs, telling their obedient conquerors what work they were to do: chop wood, prepare soup, grind coffee; one of them even was doing the washing for his hostess, an infirm old grandmother.

The count, astonished at what he saw, questioned the beadle who was coming out of the presbytery. The old man answered:

"Oh, those men are not at all a bad sort; they are not Prussians, I am told; they come from somewhere farther off, I don't exactly know where. And they have all left wives and children behind them; they are not fond of war either, you may be sure! I am sure they are mourning for the men where they come from, just as we do here; and the war causes them just as much unhappiness as it does us. As a matter of fact, things are not so very bad here just now, because the soldiers do no harm, and work just as if they were in their own homes. You see, sir, poor folk always help one another; it is the great ones of this world who make war."

Cornudet indignant at the friendly understanding established between conquerors and conquered, withdrew, preferring to shut himself up in the inn.

"They are repeopling the country," jested Loiseau.

"They are undoing the harm they have done," said Monsieur Carre-Lamadon gravely.

But they could not find the coach driver. At last he was discovered in the village cafe, fraternizing cordially with the officer's orderly.

"Were you not told to harness the horses at eight o'clock?" demanded the count.

"Oh, yes; but I've had different orders since."

"What orders?"

"Not to harness at all."

"Who gave you such orders?"

"Why, the Prussian officer."

"But why?"

"I don't know. Go and ask him. I am forbidden to harness the horses, so I don't harness them--that's all."

"Did he tell you so himself?"

"No, sir; the innkeeper gave me the order from him."

"When?"

"Last evening, just as I was going to bed."

The three men returned in a very uneasy frame of mind.

They asked for Monsieur Follenvie, but the servant replied that on account of his asthma he never got up before ten o'clock. They were strictly forbidden to rouse him earlier, except in case of fire.

They wished to see the officer, but that also was impossible, although he lodged in the inn. Monsieur Follenvie alone was authorized to interview him on civil matters. So they waited. The women returned to their rooms, and occupied themselves with trivial matters.

Cornudet settled down beside the tall kitchen fireplace, before a blazing fire. He had a small table and a jug of beer placed beside him, and he smoked his pipe--a pipe which enjoyed among democrats a consideration almost equal to his own, as though it had served its country in serving Cornudet. It was a fine meerschaum, admirably colored to a black the shade of its owner's teeth, but sweet-smelling, gracefully curved, at home in its master's hand, and completing his physiognomy. And Cornudet sat motionless, his eyes fixed now on the dancing flames, now on the froth which crowned his beer; and after each draught he passed his long, thin fingers with an air of satisfaction through his long, greasy hair, as he sucked the foam from his mustache.

Loiseau, under pretence of stretching his legs, went out to see if he could sell wine to the country dealers. The count and the manufacturer began to talk politics. They forecast the future of France. One believed in the Orleans dynasty, the other in an unknown savior--a hero who should rise up in the last extremity: a Du Guesclin, perhaps a Joan of Arc? or another Napoleon the First? Ah! if only the Prince Imperial were not so young! Cornudet, listening to them, smiled like a man who holds the keys of destiny in his hands. His pipe perfumed the whole kitchen.

As the clock struck ten, Monsieur Follenvie appeared. He was immediately surrounded and questioned, but could only repeat, three or four times in succession, and without variation, the words:

"The officer said to me, just like this: 'Monsieur Follenvie, you will forbid them to harness up the coach for those travellers to-morrow. They are not to start without an order from me. You hear? That is sufficient.'"

Then they asked to see the officer. The count sent him his card, on which Monsieur Carre-Lamadon also inscribed his name and titles. The Prussian sent word that the two men would be admitted to see him after his luncheon--that is to say, about one o'clock.

The ladies reappeared, and they all ate a little, in spite of their anxiety. Boule de Suif appeared ill and very much worried.

They were finishing their coffee when the orderly came to fetch the gentlemen.

Loiseau joined the other two; but when they tried to get Cornudet to accompany them, by way of adding greater solemnity to the occasion, he declared proudly that he would never have anything to do with the Germans, and, resuming his seat in the chimney corner, he called for another jug of beer.

The three men went upstairs, and were ushered into the best room in the inn, where the officer received them lolling at his ease in an armchair, his feet on the mantelpiece, smoking a long porcelain pipe, and enveloped in a gorgeous dressing-gown, doubtless stolen from the deserted dwelling of some citizen destitute of taste in dress. He neither rose, greeted them, nor even glanced in their direction. He afforded a fine example of that insolence of bearing which seems natural to the victorious soldier.

After the lapse of a few moments he said in his halting French:

"What do you want?"

"We wish to start on our journey," said the count.

"No."

"May I ask the reason of your refusal?"

"Because I don't choose."

"I would respectfully call your attention, monsieur, to the fact that your general in command gave us a permit to proceed to Dieppe; and I do not think we have done anything to deserve this harshness at your hands."

"I don't choose--that's all. You may go."

They bowed, and retired.

The afternoon was wretched. They could not understand the caprice of this German, and the strangest ideas came into their heads. They all congregated in the kitchen, and talked the subject to death, imagining all kinds of unlikely things. Perhaps they were to be kept as hostages --but for what reason? or to be extradited as prisoners of war? or possibly they were to be held for ransom? They were panic-stricken at this last supposition. The richest among them were the most alarmed, seeing themselves forced to empty bags of gold into the insolent soldier's hands in order to buy back their lives. They racked their brains for plausible lies whereby they might conceal the fact that they were rich, and pass themselves off as poor--very poor. Loiseau took off his watch chain, and put it in his pocket. The approach of night increased their apprehension. The lamp was lighted, and as it wanted yet two hours to dinner

Madame Loiseau proposed a game of trente et un. It would distract their thoughts. The rest agreed, and Cornudet himself joined the party, first putting out his pipe for politeness' sake.

The count shuffled the cards--dealt--and Boule de Suif had thirty-one to start with; soon the interest of the game assuaged the anxiety of the players. But Cornudet noticed that Loiseau and his wife were in league to cheat.

They were about to sit down to dinner when Monsieur Follenvie appeared, and in his grating voice announced:

"The Prussian officer sends to ask Mademoiselle Elisabeth Rousset if she has changed her mind yet."

Boule de Suif stood still, pale as death. Then, suddenly turning crimson with anger, she gasped out:

"Kindly tell that scoundrel, that cur, that carrion of a Prussian, that I will never consent--you understand?--never, never, never!"

The fat innkeeper left the room. Then Boule de Suif was surrounded, questioned, entreated on all sides to reveal the mystery of her visit to the officer. She refused at first; but her wrath soon got the better of her.

"What does he want? He wants to make me his mistress!" she cried.

No one was shocked at the word, so great was the general indignation. Cornudet broke his jug as he banged it down on the table. A loud outcry arose against this base soldier. All were furious. They drew together in common resistance against the foe, as if some part of the sacrifice exacted of Boule de Suif had been demanded of each. The count declared, with supreme disgust, that those people behaved like ancient barbarians. The women, above all, manifested a lively and tender sympathy for Boule de Suif. The nuns, who appeared only at meals, cast down their eyes, and said nothing.

They dined, however, as soon as the first indignant outburst had subsided; but they spoke little and thought much.

The ladies went to bed early; and the men, having lighted their pipes, proposed a game of ecarte, in which Monsieur Follenvie was invited to join, the travellers hoping to question him skillfully as to the best means of vanquishing the officer's obduracy. But he thought of nothing but his cards, would listen to nothing, reply to nothing, and repeated, time after time: "Attend to the game, gentlemen! attend to the game!" So absorbed was his attention that he even forgot to expectorate. The consequence was that his chest gave forth rumbling sounds like those of an organ. His wheezing lungs struck every note of the asthmatic scale, from deep, hollow tones to a shrill, hoarse piping resembling that of a young cock trying to crow.

He refused to go to bed when his wife, overcome with sleep, came to fetch him. So she went off alone, for she was an early bird, always up with the sun; while he was addicted to late hours, ever ready to spend the night with friends. He merely said: "Put my egg-nogg by the fire," and went on with the game. When the other men saw that nothing was to be got out of him they declared it was time to retire, and each sought his bed.

They rose fairly early the next morning, with a vague hope of being allowed to start, a greater desire than ever to do so, and a terror at having to spend another day in this wretched little inn.

Alas! the horses remained in the stable, the driver was invisible. They spent their time, for want of something better to do, in wandering round the coach.

Luncheon was a gloomy affair; and there was a general coolness toward Boule de Suif, for night, which brings counsel, had somewhat modified the judgment of her companions. In the cold light of the morning they almost bore a grudge against the girl for not having secretly sought out the Prussian, that the rest of the party might receive a joyful surprise when they awoke. What more simple?

Besides, who would have been the wiser? She might have saved appearances by telling the officer that she had taken pity on their distress. Such a step would be of so little consequence to her.

But no one as yet confessed to such thoughts.

In the afternoon, seeing that they were all bored to death, the count proposed a walk in the neighborhood of the village. Each one wrapped himself up well, and the little party set out, leaving behind only Cornudet, who preferred to sit over the fire, and the two nuns, who were in the habit of spending their day in the church or at the presbytery.

The cold, which grew more intense each day, almost froze the noses and ears of the pedestrians, their feet began to pain them so that each step was a penance, and when they reached the open country it looked so mournful and depressing in its limitless mantle of white that they all hastily retraced their steps, with bodies benumbed and hearts heavy.

The four women walked in front, and the three men followed a little in their rear.

Loiseau, who saw perfectly well how matters stood, asked suddenly "if that trollop were going to keep them waiting much longer in this Godforsaken spot." The count, always courteous, replied that they could not exact so painful a sacrifice from any woman, and that the first move must come from herself. Monsieur Carre-Lamadon remarked that if the French, as they talked of doing, made a counter attack by way of Dieppe, their encounter with the enemy must inevitably take place at Totes. This reflection made the other two anxious.

"Supposing we escape on foot?" said Loiseau.

The count shrugged his shoulders.

"How can you think of such a thing, in this snow? And with our wives? Besides, we should be pursued at once, overtaken in ten minutes, and brought back as prisoners at the mercy of the soldiery."

This was true enough; they were silent.

The ladies talked of dress, but a certain constraint seemed to prevail among them.

Suddenly, at the end of the street, the officer appeared. His tall, wasp-like, uniformed figure was outlined against the snow which bounded the horizon, and he walked, knees apart, with that motion peculiar to soldiers, who are always anxious not to soil their carefully polished boots.

He bowed as he passed the ladies, then glanced scornfully at the men, who had sufficient dignity not to raise their hats, though Loiseau made a movement to do so.

Boule de Suif flushed crimson to the ears, and the three married women felt unutterably humiliated at being met thus by the soldier in company with the girl whom he had treated with such scant ceremony.

Then they began to talk about him, his figure, and his face. Madame Carré-Lamadon, who had known many officers and judged them as a connoisseur, thought him not at all bad-looking; she even regretted that he was not a Frenchman, because in that case he would have made a very handsome hussar, with whom all the women would assuredly have fallen in love.

When they were once more within doors they did not know what to do with themselves. Sharp words even were exchanged apropos of the merest trifles. The silent dinner was quickly over, and each one went to bed early in the hope of sleeping, and thus killing time.

They came down next morning with tired faces and irritable tempers; the women scarcely spoke to Boule de Suif.

A church bell summoned the faithful to a baptism. Boule de Suif had a child being brought up by peasants at Yvetot. She did not see him once a year, and never thought of him; but the idea of the child who was about to be baptized induced a sudden wave of tenderness for her own, and she insisted on being present at the ceremony.

As soon as she had gone out, the rest of the company looked at one another and then drew their chairs together; for they realized that they must decide on some course of action. Loiseau had an inspiration: he proposed that they should ask the officer to detain Boule de Suif only, and to let the rest depart on their way.

Monsieur Follenvie was intrusted with this commission, but he returned to them almost immediately. The German, who knew human nature, had shown him the door. He intended to keep all the travellers until his condition had been complied with.

Whereupon Madame Loiseau's vulgar temperament broke bounds.

"We're not going to die of old age here!" she cried. "Since it's that vixen's trade to behave so with men I don't see that she has any right to refuse one more than another. I may as well tell you she took any lovers she could get at Rouen-- even coachmen! Yes, indeed, madame--the coachman at the prefecture! I know it for a fact, for he buys his wine of us. And now that it is a question of getting us out of a difficulty she puts on virtuous airs, the drab! For my part, I think this officer has behaved very well. Why, there were three others of us, any one of whom he would undoubtedly have preferred. But no, he contents himself with the girl who is common property. He respects married women. Just think. He is master here. He had only to say: 'I wish it!' and he might have taken us by force, with the help of his soldiers."

The two other women shuddered; the eyes of pretty Madame Carre-Lamadon glistened, and she grew pale, as if the officer were indeed in the act of laying violent hands on her.

The men, who had been discussing the subject among themselves, drew near. Loiseau, in a state of furious resentment, was for delivering up "that miserable woman," bound hand and foot, into the enemy's power. But the count, descended from three generations of ambassadors, and endowed, moreover, with the lineaments of a diplomat, was in favor of more tactful measures.

"We must persuade her," he said.

Then they laid their plans.

The women drew together; they lowered their voices, and the discussion became general, each giving his or her opinion. But the conversation was not in the least coarse. The ladies, in particular, were adepts at delicate phrases and charming subtleties of expression to describe the most improper things. A stranger would have understood none of their allusions, so guarded was the language they employed. But, seeing that the thin veneer of modesty with which every woman of the world is furnished goes but a very little way below the surface, they began rather to enjoy this unedifying episode, and at bottom were hugely delighted-- feeling themselves in their element, furthering the schemes of lawless love with the gusto of a gourmand cook who prepares supper for another.

Their gaiety returned of itself, so amusing at last did the whole business seem to them. The count uttered several rather risky witticisms, but so tactfully were they said that his audience could not help smiling. Loiseau in turn made some considerably broader jokes, but no one took offence; and the thought expressed with such brutal directness by his wife was uppermost in the minds of all: "Since it's the girl's trade, why should she refuse this man more than another?"

Dainty Madame Carre-Lamadon seemed to think even that in Boule de Suif's place she would be less inclined to refuse him than another.

The blockade was as carefully arranged as if they were investing a fortress. Each agreed on the role which he or she was to play, the arguments to be used, the maneuvers to be executed. They decided on the plan of campaign, the stratagems they were to employ, and the surprise attacks which were to reduce this human citadel and force it to receive the enemy within its walls.

But Cornudet remained apart from the rest, taking no share in the plot.

So absorbed was the attention of all that Boule de Suif's entrance was almost unnoticed. But the count whispered a gentle "Hush!" which made the others look up. She was there. They suddenly stopped talking, and a vague embarrassment prevented them for a few moments from addressing her. But the countess, more practiced than the others in the wiles of the drawing-room, asked her:

"Was the baptism interesting?"

The girl, still under the stress of emotion, told what she had seen and heard, described the faces, the attitudes of those present, and even the appearance of the church. She concluded with the words:

"It does one good to pray sometimes."

Until lunch time the ladies contented themselves with being pleasant to her, so as to increase her confidence and make her amenable to their advice.

As soon as they took their seats at table the attack began. First they opened a vague conversation on the subject of self-sacrifice. Ancient examples were quoted: Judith and Holofernes; then, irrationally enough, Lucrece and Sextus; Cleopatra and the hostile generals whom she reduced to abject slavery by a surrender of her charms. Next was recounted an extraordinary story, born of the imagination of these ignorant millionaires, which told how the matrons of Rome seduced Hannibal, his lieutenants, and all his mercenaries at Capua. They held up to admiration all those women who from time to time have arrested the victorious progress of conquerors, made of their bodies a field of battle, a means of ruling, a weapon; who have vanquished by their heroic caresses hideous or detested beings, and sacrificed their chastity to vengeance and devotion.

All was said with due restraint and regard for propriety, the effect heightened now and then by an outburst of forced enthusiasm calculated to excite emulation.

A listener would have thought at last that the one role of woman on earth was a perpetual sacrifice of her person, a continual abandonment of herself to the caprices of a hostile soldiery.

The two nuns seemed to hear nothing, and to be lost in thought. Boule de Suif also was silent.

During the whole afternoon she was left to her reflections. But instead of calling her "madame" as they had done hitherto, her companions addressed her simply as "mademoiselle," without exactly knowing why, but as if desirous of making her descend a step in the esteem she had won, and forcing her to realize her degraded position.

Just as soup was served, Monsieur Follenvie reappeared, repeating his phrase of the evening before:

"The Prussian officer sends to ask if Mademoiselle Elisabeth Rousset has changed her mind."

Boule de Suif answered briefly:

"No, monsieur."

But at dinner the coalition weakened. Loiseau made three unfortunate remarks. Each was cudgeling his brains for further examples of self-sacrifice, and could find none, when the countess, possibly without ulterior motive, and moved simply by a vague desire to do homage to religion, began to question the elder of the two nuns on the most striking facts in the lives of the saints. Now, it fell out that many of these had committed acts which would be crimes in our eyes, but the Church readily pardons such deeds when they are accomplished for the glory of God or the good of mankind. This was a powerful argument, and the countess made the most of it. Then, whether by reason of a tacit understanding, a thinly veiled act of complaisance such as those who wear the ecclesiastical habit excel in, or whether merely as the result of sheer stupidity--a stupidity admirably adapted to further their designs-- the old nun rendered formidable aid to the conspirator. They had thought her timid; she proved herself bold, talkative, bigoted. She was not troubled by the ins and outs of casuistry; her doctrines were as iron bars; her faith knew no doubt; her conscience no scruples. She looked on Abraham's sacrifice as natural enough, for she herself would not have hesitated to kill both father and mother if she had received a divine order to that effect; and nothing, in her opinion, could displease our Lord, provided the motive were praiseworthy. The countess, putting to good use the consecrated authority of her unexpected ally, led her on to make a lengthy and edifying paraphrase of that axiom enunciated by a certain school of moralists: "The end justifies the means."

"Then, sister," she asked, "you think God accepts all methods, and pardons the act when the motive is pure?"

"Undoubtedly, madame. An action reprehensible in itself often derives merit from the thought which inspires it."

And in this wise they talked on, fathoming the wishes of God, predicting His judgments, describing Him as interested in matters which assuredly concern Him but little.

All was said with the utmost care and discretion, but every word uttered by the holy woman in her nun's garb weakened the indignant resistance of the courtesan. Then the conversation drifted somewhat, and the nun began to talk of the convents of her order, of her Superior, of herself, and of her fragile little neighbor, Sister St. Nicephore. They had been sent for from Havre to nurse the hundreds of soldiers who were in hospitals, stricken with smallpox. She described these wretched invalids and their malady. And, while they themselves were detained on their way by the caprices of the Prussian officer, scores of Frenchmen might be dying, whom they would otherwise have saved! For the nursing of soldiers was the old nun's specialty; she had been in the Crimea, in Italy, in Austria; and as she told the story of her campaigns she revealed herself as one of those holy sisters of the fife and drum who seem designed by nature to follow camps, to snatch the wounded from amid the strife of battle, and to quell with a word, more effectually than any general, the rough and insubordinate troopers--a masterful woman, her seamed and pitted face itself an image of the devastations of war.

No one spoke when she had finished for fear of spoiling the excellent effect of her words.

As soon as the meal was over the travellers retired to their rooms, whence they emerged the following day at a late hour of the morning.

Luncheon passed off quietly. The seed sown the preceding evening was being given time to germinate and bring forth fruit.

In the afternoon the countess proposed a walk; then the count, as had been arranged beforehand, took Boule de Suif's arm, and walked with her at some distance behind the rest.

He began talking to her in that familiar, paternal, slightly contemptuous tone which men of his class adopt in speaking to women like her, calling her "my dear child," and talking down to her from the height of his exalted social position and stainless reputation. He came straight to the point.

"So you prefer to leave us here, exposed like yourself to all the violence which would follow on a repulse of the Prussian troops, rather than consent to surrender yourself, as you have done so many times in your life?"

The girl did not reply.

He tried kindness, argument, sentiment. He still bore himself as count, even while adopting, when desirable, an attitude of gallantry, and making pretty-- nay, even tender--speeches. He exalted the service she would render them, spoke of their gratitude; then, suddenly, using the familiar "thou":

"And you know, my dear, he could boast then of having made a conquest of a pretty girl such as he won't often find in his own country."

Boule de Suif did not answer, and joined the rest of the party.

As soon as they returned she went to her room, and was seen no more. The general anxiety was at its height. What would she do? If she still resisted, how awkward for them all!

The dinner hour struck; they waited for her in vain. At last Monsieur Follenvie entered, announcing that Mademoiselle Rousset was not well, and that they might sit down to table. They all pricked up their ears. The count drew near the innkeeper, and whispered:

"Is it all right?"

"Yes."

Out of regard for propriety he said nothing to his companions, but merely nodded slightly toward them. A great sigh of relief went up from all breasts; every face was lighted up with joy.

"By Gad!" shouted Loiseau, "I'll stand champagne all round if there's any to be found in this place." And great was Madame Loiseau's dismay when the proprietor came back with four bottles in his hands. They had all suddenly become talkative and merry; a lively joy filled all hearts. The count seemed to perceive for the first time that Madame Carre-Lamadon was charming; the manufacturer paid compliments to the countess. The conversation was animated, sprightly, witty, and, although many of the jokes were in the worst possible taste, all the company were amused by them, and none offended-- indignation being dependent, like other emotions, on surroundings. And the mental atmosphere had gradually become filled with gross imaginings and unclean thoughts.

At dessert even the women indulged in discreetly worded allusions. Their glances were full of meaning; they had drunk much. The count, who even in his moments of relaxation preserved a dignified demeanor, hit on a much-appreciated comparison of the condition of things with the termination of a winter spent in the icy solitude of the North Pole and the joy of shipwrecked mariners who at last perceive a southward track opening out before their eyes.

Loiseau, fairly in his element, rose to his feet, holding aloft a glass of champagne.

"I drink to our deliverance!" he shouted.

All stood up, and greeted the toast with acclamation. Even the two good sisters yielded to the solicitations of the ladies, and consented to moisten their lips with the foaming wine, which they had never before tasted. They declared it was like effervescent lemonade, but with a pleasanter flavor.

"It is a pity," said Loiseau, "that we have no piano; we might have had a quadrille."

Cornudet had not spoken a word or made a movement; he seemed plunged in serious thought, and now and then tugged furiously at his great beard, as if trying to add still further to its length. At last, toward midnight, when they were about to separate, Loiseau, whose gait was far from steady, suddenly slapped him on the back, saying thickly:

"You're not jolly to-night; why are you so silent, old man?"

Cornudet threw back his head, cast one swift and scornful glance over the assemblage, and answered:

"I tell you all, you have done an infamous thing!"

He rose, reached the door, and repeating: "Infamous!" disappeared.

A chill fell on all. Loiseau himself looked foolish and disconcerted for a moment, but soon recovered his aplomb, and, writhing with laughter, exclaimed:

"Really, you are all too green for anything!"

Pressed for an explanation, he related the "mysteries of the corridor," whereat his listeners were hugely amused. The ladies could hardly contain their delight. The count and Monsieur Carre-Lamadon laughed till they cried. They could scarcely believe their ears.

"What! you are sure? He wanted----"

"I tell you I saw it with my own eyes."

"And she refused?"

"Because the Prussian was in the next room!"

"Surely you are mistaken?"

"I swear I'm telling you the truth."

The count was choking with laughter. The manufacturer held his sides. Loiseau continued:

"So you may well imagine he doesn't think this evening's business at all amusing."

And all three began to laugh again, choking, coughing, almost ill with merriment.

Then they separated. But Madame Loiseau, who was nothing if not spiteful, remarked to her husband as they were on the way to bed that "that stuck-up little minx of a Carre-Lamadon had laughed on the wrong side of her mouth all the evening."

"You know," she said, "when women run after uniforms it's all the same to them whether the men who wear them are French or Prussian. It's perfectly sickening!"

The next morning the snow showed dazzling white tinder a clear winter sun. The coach, ready at last, waited before the door; while a flock of white pigeons, with pink eyes spotted in the centres with black, puffed out their white feathers and walked sedately between the legs of the six horses, picking at the steaming manure.

The driver, wrapped in his sheepskin coat, was smoking a pipe on the box, and all the passengers, radiant with delight at their approaching departure, were putting up provisions for the remainder of the journey.

They were waiting only for Boule de Suif. At last she appeared.

She seemed rather shamefaced and embarrassed, and advanced with timid step toward her companions, who with one accord turned aside as if they had not seen her. The count, with much dignity, took his wife by the arm, and removed her from the unclean contact.

The girl stood still, stupefied with astonishment; then, plucking up courage, accosted the manufacturer's wife with a humble "Good-morning, madame," to which the other replied merely with a slight arid insolent nod, accompanied by a look of outraged virtue. Every one suddenly appeared extremely busy, and kept as far from Boule de Suif as if tier skirts had been infected with some deadly disease. Then they hurried to the coach, followed by the despised courtesan, who, arriving last of all, silently took the place she had occupied during the first part of the journey.

The rest seemed neither to see nor to know her--all save Madame Loiseau, who, glancing contemptuously in her direction, remarked, half aloud, to her husband:

"What a mercy I am not sitting beside that creature!"

The lumbering vehicle started on its way, and the journey began afresh.

At first no one spoke. Boule de Suif dared not even raise her eyes. She felt at once indignant with her neighbors, and humiliated at having yielded to the Prussian into whose arms they had so hypocritically cast her.

But the countess, turning toward Madame Carre-Lamadon, soon broke the painful silence:

"I think you know Madame d'Etrelles?"

"Yes; she is a friend of mine."

"Such a charming woman!"

"Delightful! Exceptionally talented, and an artist to the finger tips. She sings marvellously and draws to perfection."

The manufacturer was chatting with the count, and amid the clatter of the window-panes a word of their conversation was now and then distinguishable: "Shares--maturity--premium--time-limit."

Loiseau, who had abstracted from the inn the timeworn pack of cards, thick with the grease of five years' contact with half-wiped-off tables, started a game of bezique with his wife.

The good sisters, taking up simultaneously the long rosaries hanging from their waists, made the sign of the cross, and began to mutter in unison interminable prayers, their lips moving ever more and more swiftly, as if they sought which should outdistance the other in the race of orisons; from time to time they kissed a medal, and crossed themselves anew, then resumed their rapid and unintelligible murmur.

Cornudet sat still, lost in thought.

Ah the end of three hours Loiseau gathered up the cards, and remarked that he was hungry.

His wife thereupon produced a parcel tied with string, from which she extracted a piece of cold veal. This she cut into neat, thin slices, and both began to eat.

"We may as well do the same," said the countess. The rest agreed, and she unpacked the provisions which had been prepared for herself, the count, and the Carre-Lamadons. In one of those oval dishes, the lids of which are decorated with an earthenware hare, by way of showing that a game pie lies within, was a succulent delicacy consisting of the brown flesh of the game larded with streaks of bacon and flavored with other meats chopped fine. A solid wedge of Gruyere cheese, which had been wrapped in a newspaper, bore the imprint: "Items of News," on its rich, oily surface.

The two good sisters brought to light a hunk of sausage smelling strongly of garlic; and Cornudet, plunging both hands at once into the capacious pockets of his loose overcoat, produced from one four hard-boiled eggs and from the other a crust of bread. He removed the shells, threw them into the straw beneath his feet, and began to devour the eggs, letting morsels of the bright yellow yolk fall in his mighty beard, where they looked like stars.

Boule de Suif, in the haste and confusion of her departure, had not thought of anything, and, stifling with rage, she watched all these people placidly eating. At first, ill-suppressed wrath shook her whole person, and she opened her lips to shriek the truth at them, to overwhelm them with a volley of insults; but she could not utter a word, so choked was she with indignation.

No one looked at her, no one thought of her. She felt herself swallowed up in the scorn of these virtuous creatures, who had first sacrificed, then rejected her as a thing useless and unclean. Then she remembered her big basket full of the good things they had so greedily devoured: the two chickens coated in jelly, the pies, the pears, the four bottles of claret; and her fury broke forth like a cord that is overstrained, and she was on the verge of tears. She made terrible efforts at self- control, drew herself up, swallowed the sobs which choked her; but the tears rose nevertheless, shone at the brink of her eyelids, and soon two heavy drops coursed slowly down her cheeks. Others followed more quickly, like water filtering from a rock, and fell, one after another, on her rounded bosom. She sat upright, with a fixed expression, her face pale and rigid, hoping desperately that no one saw her give way.

But the countess noticed that she was weeping, and with a sign drew her husband's attention to the fact. He shrugged his shoulders, as if to say: "Well, what of it? It's not my fault." Madame Loiseau chuckled triumphantly, and murmured:

"She's weeping for shame."

The two nuns had betaken themselves once more to their prayers, first wrapping the remainder of their sausage in paper:

Then Cornudet, who was digesting his eggs, stretched his long legs under the opposite seat, threw himself back, folded his arms, smiled like a man who had just thought of a good joke, and began to whistle the Marseillaise.

The faces of his neighbors clouded; the popular air evidently did not find favor with them; they grew nervous and irritable, and seemed ready to howl as a dog does at the sound of a barrel-organ. Cornudet saw the discomfort he was creating, and whistled the louder; sometimes he even hummed the words:

Amour sacre de la patrie, Conduis, soutiens, nos bras vengeurs, Liberte, liberte cherie, Combats avec tes defenseurs!

The coach progressed more swiftly, the snow being harder now; and all the way to Dieppe, during the long, dreary hours of the journey, first in the gathering dusk, then in the thick darkness, raising his voice above the rumbling of the vehicle, Cornudet continued with fierce obstinacy his vengeful and monotonous whistling, forcing his weary and exasperated- hearers to follow the song from end to end, to recall every word of every line, as each was repeated over and over again with untiring persistency.

And Boule de Suif still wept, and sometimes a sob she could not restrain was heard in the darkness between two verses of the song.

THE HORLA

MAY 8. What a lovely day! I have spent all the morning lying on the grass in front of my house, under the enormous plantain tree which covers and shades and shelters the whole of it. I like this part of the country; I am fond of living here because I am attached to it by deep roots, the profound and delicate roots which attach a man to the soil on which his ancestors were born and died, to their traditions, their usages, their food, the local expressions, the peculiar language of the peasants, the smell of the soil, the hamlets, and to the atmosphere itself.

I love the house in which I grew up. From my windows I can see the Seine, which flows by the side of my garden, on the other side of the road, almost through my grounds, the great and wide Seine, which goes to Rouen and Havre, and which is covered with boats passing to and fro.

On the left, down yonder, lies Rouen, populous Rouen with its blue roofs massing under pointed, Gothic towers. Innumerable are they, delicate or broad, dominated by the spire of the cathedral, full of bells which sound through the blue air on fine mornings, sending their sweet and distant Iron clang to me, their metallic sounds, now stronger and now weaker, according as the wind is strong or light.

What a delicious morning it was! About eleven o'clock, a long line of boats drawn by a steam-tug, as big a fly, and which scarcely puffed while emitting its thick smoke, passed my gate.

After two English schooners, whose red flags fluttered toward the sky, there came a magnificent Brazilian three-master; it was perfectly white and wonderfully clean and shining. I saluted it, I hardly know why, except that the sight of the vessel gave me great pleasure.

May 12. I have had a slight feverish attack for the last few days, and I feel ill, or rather I feel low-spirited.

Whence come those mysterious influences which change our happiness into discouragement, and our self-confidence into diffidence? One might almost say that the air, the invisible air, is full of unknowable Forces, whose mysterious presence we have to endure. I wake up in the best of spirits, with an inclination

105

to sing in my heart. Why? I go down by the side of the water, and suddenly, after walking a short distance, I return home wretched, as If some misfortune were awaiting me there. Why? Is it a cold shiver which, passing over my skin, has upset my nerves and given me a fit of low spirits? Is it the form of the clouds, or the tints of the sky, or the colors of the surrounding objects which are so changeable, which have troubled my thoughts as they passed before my eyes? Who can tell? Everything that surrounds us, everything that we see without looking at it, everything that we touch without knowing it, everything that we handle without feeling it, everything that we meet without clearly distinguishing it, has a rapid, surprising, and inexplicable effect upon us and upon our organs, and through them on our ideas and on our being itself.

How profound that mystery of the Invisible is! We cannot fathom it with our miserable senses: our eyes are unable to perceive what is either too small or too great, too near to or too far from us; we can see neither the inhabitants of a star nor of a drop of water; our ears deceive us, for they transmit to us the vibrations of the air in sonorous notes. Our senses are fairies who work the miracle of changing that movement into noise, and by that metamorphosis give birth to music, which makes the mute agitation of nature a harmony. So with our sense of smell, which is weaker than that of a dog, and so with our sense of taste, which can scarcely distinguish the age of a wine!

Oh! If we only had other organs which could work other miracles in our favor, what a number of fresh things we might discover around us!

May 16. I am ill, decidedly! I was so well last month! I am feverish, horribly feverish, or rather I am in a state of feverish enervation, which makes my mind suffer as much as my body. I have without ceasing the horrible sensation of some danger threatening me, the apprehension of some coming misfortune or of approaching death, a presentiment which is no doubt, an attack of some illness still unnamed, which germinates in the flesh and in the blood.

May 18. I have just come from consulting my medical man, for I can no longer get any sleep. He found that my pulse was high, my eyes dilated, my nerves highly strung, but no alarming symptoms. I must have a course of shower baths and of bromide of potassium.

May 25. No change! My state is really very peculiar. As the evening comes on, an incomprehensible feeling of disquietude seizes me, just as if night concealed some terrible menace toward me. I dine quickly, and then try to read, but I do not understand the words, and can scarcely distinguish the letters. Then I walk up and down my drawing-room, oppressed by a feeling of confused and irresistible fear, a fear of sleep and a fear of my bed.

About ten o'clock I go up to my room. As soon as I have entered I lock and bolt the door. I am frightened -- of what? Up till the present time I have been frightened of nothing. I open my cupboards, and look under my bed; I listen -- I listen -- to what? How strange it is that a simple feeling of discomfort, of impeded or heightened circulation, perhaps the irritation of a nervous center, a slight congestion, a small disturbance in the imperfect and delicate functions of our living machinery, can turn the most light-hearted of men into a melancholy one, and make a coward of the bravest? Then, I go to bed, and I wait for sleep as a man might wait for the executioner. I wait for its coming with dread, and my heart beats and my legs tremble, while my whole body shivers beneath the warmth of the bedclothes, until the moment when I suddenly fall asleep, as a man throws himself into a pool of stagnant water in order to drown. I do not feel this perfidious sleep coming over me as I used to, but a sleep which is close to me and watching me, which is going to seize me by the head, to close my eyes and annihilate me.

I sleep -- a long time -- two or three hours perhaps -- then a dream -- no -- a nightmare lays hold on me. I feel that I am in bed and asleep -- I feel it and I know it -- and I feel also that somebody is coming close to me, is looking at me, touching me, is getting on to my bed, is kneeling on my chest, is taking my neck between his hands and squeezing it -- squeezing it with all his might in order to strangle me.

I struggle, bound by that terrible powerlessness which paralyzes us in our dreams; I try to cry out -- but I cannot; I want to move -- I cannot; I try, with the most violent efforts and out of breath, to turn over and throw off this being which is crushing and suffocating me -- I cannot!

And then suddenly I wake up, shaken and bathed in perspiration; I light a candle and find that I am alone, and after that crisis, which occurs every night, I at length fall asleep and slumber tranquilly till morning.

June 2. My state has grown worse. What is the matter with me? The bromide does me no good, and the shower-baths have no effect whatever. Sometimes, in order to tire myself out, though I am fatigued enough already, I go for a walk in the forest of Roumare. I used to think at first that the fresh light and soft air, impregnated with the odor of herbs and leaves, would instill new life into my veins and impart fresh energy to my heart. One day I turned into a broad ride in the wood, and then I diverged toward La Bouille, through a narrow path, between two rows of exceedingly tall trees, which placed a thick, green, almost black roof between the sky and me.

A sudden shiver ran through me, not a cold shiver, but a shiver of agony, and so I hastened my steps, uneasy at being alone in the wood, frightened stupidly and without reason, at the profound solitude. Suddenly it seemed as if I were being followed, that somebody was walking at my heels, close, quite close to me, near enough to touch me.

107

I turned round suddenly, but I was alone. I saw nothing behind me except the straight, broad ride, empty and bordered by high trees, horribly empty; on the other side also it extended until it was lost in the distance, and looked just the same -- terrible.

I closed my eyes. Why? And then I began to turn round on one heel very quickly, just like a top. I nearly fell down, and opened my eyes; the trees were dancing round me and the earth heaved; I was obliged to sit down. Then, ah! I no longer remembered how I had come! What a strange idea! What a strange, strange idea! I did not the least know. I started off to the right, and got back into the avenue which had led me into the middle of the forest.

June 3. I have had a terrible night. I shall go away for a few weeks, for no doubt a journey will set me up again.

July 2. I have come back, quite cured, and have had a most delightful trip into the bargain. I have been to Mont Saint-Michel, which I had not seen before.

What a sight, when one arrives as I did, at Avranches toward the end of the day! The town stands on a hill, and I was taken into the public garden at the extremity of the town. I uttered a cry of astonishment. An extraordinarily large bay lay extended before me, as far as my eyes could reach, between two hills which were lost to sight in the mist; and in the middle of this immense yellow bay, under a clear, golden sky, a peculiar hill rose up, somber and pointed in the midst of the sand. The sun had just disappeared, and under the still flaming sky stood out the outline of that fantastic rock which bears on its summit a picturesque monument.

At daybreak I went to it. The tide was low, as it had been the night before, and I saw that wonderful abbey rise up before me as I approached it. After several hours' walking, I reached the enormous mass of rock which supports the little town, dominated by the great church. Having climbed the steep and narrow street, I entered the most wonderful Gothic building that has ever been erected to God on earth, large as a town, and full of low rooms which seem buried beneath vaulted roofs, and of lofty galleries supported by delicate columns.

I entered this gigantic granite jewel, which is as light in its effect as a bit of lace and is covered with towers, with slender belfries to which spiral staircases ascend. The flying buttresses raise strange heads that bristle with chimeras. with devils, with fantastic animals, with monstrous flowers, are joined together by finely carved arches, to the blue sky by day, and to the black sky by night.

When I had reached the summit. I said to the monk who accompanied me: ``Father, how happy you must be here!" And he replied: ``It is very windy,

Monsieur"; and so we began to talk while watching the rising tide, which ran over the sand and covered it with a steel cuirass.

And then the monk told me stories, all the old stories belonging to the place -- legends, nothing but legends.

One of them struck me forcibly. The country people, those belonging to the Mornet, declare that at night one can hear talking going on in the sand, and also that two goats bleat, one with a strong, the other with a weak voice. Incredulous people declare that it is nothing but the screaming of the sea birds, which occasionally resembles bleatings, and occasionally human lamentations; but belated fishermen swear that they have met an old shepherd, whose cloak covered head they can never see, wandering on the sand, between two tides, round the little town placed so far out of the world. They declare he is guiding and walking before a he-goat with a man's face and a she-goat with a woman's face, both with white hair, who talk incessantly, quarreling in a strange language, and then suddenly cease talking in order to bleat with all their might.

``Do you believe it?" I asked the monk. ``I scarcely know," he replied; and I continued: ``If there are other beings besides ourselves on this earth, how comes it that we have not known it for so long a time, or why have you not seen them? How is it that I have not seen them?"

He replied: ``Do we see the hundred-thousandth part of what exists? Look here; there is the wind, which is the strongest force in nature. It knocks down men, and blows down buildings, uproots trees, raises the sea into mountains of water, destroys cliffs and casts great ships on to the breakers; it kills, it whistles, it sighs, it roars. But have you ever seen it, and can you see it? Yet it exists for all that."

I was silent before this simple reasoning. That man was a philosopher, or perhaps a fool; I could not say which exactly, so I held my tongue. What he had said had often been in my own thoughts.

July 3. I have slept badly; certainly there is some feverish influence here, for my coachman is suffering in the same way as I am. When I went back home yesterday, I noticed his singular paleness, and I asked him: ``What is the matter with you, Jean?"

``The matter is that I never get any rest, and my nights devour my days. Since your departure, Monsieur, there has been a spell over me."

However, the other servants are all well, but I am very frightened of having another attack, myself.

July 4. I am decidedly taken again; for my old nightmares have returned. Last night I felt somebody leaning on me who was sucking my life from between my lips with his mouth. Yes, he was sucking it out of my neck like a leech would have done. Then he got up, satiated, and I woke up, so beaten, crushed, and annihilated that I could not move. If this continues for a few days, I shall certainly go away again.

July 5. Have I lost my reason? What has happened? What I saw last night is so strange that my head wanders when I think of it!

As I do now every evening, I had locked my door; then, being thirsty, I drank half a glass of water, and I accidentally noticed that the water-bottle was full up to the cut-glass stopper.

Then I went to bed and fell into one of my terrible sleeps, from which I was aroused in about two hours by a still more terrible shock.

Picture to yourself a sleeping man who is being murdered, who wakes up with a knife in his chest, a gurgling in his throat, is covered with blood, can no longer breathe, is going to die and does not understand anything at all about it -- there you have it.

Having recovered my senses, I was thirsty again, so I lighted a candle and went to the table on which my water-bottle was. I lifted it up and tilted it over my glass, but nothing came out. It was empty! It was completely empty! At first I could not understand it at all; then suddenly I was seized by such a terrible feeling that I had to sit down, or rather fall into a chair! Then I sprang up with a bound to look about me; then I sat down again, overcome by astonishment and fear, in front of the transparent crystal bottle! I looked at it with fixed eyes, trying to solve the puzzle, and my hands trembled! Some body had drunk the water, but who? I? I without any doubt. It could surely only be I? In that case I was a somnambulist -- was living, without knowing it, that double, mysterious life which makes us doubt whether there are not two beings in us -- whether a strange, unknowable, and invisible being does not, during our moments of mental and physical torpor, animate the inert body, forcing it to a more willing obedience than it yields to ourselves.

Oh! Who will understand my horrible agony? Who will understand the emotion of a man sound in mind, wide-awake, full of sense, who looks in horror at the disappearance of a little water while he was asleep, through the glass of a water-bottle! And I remained sitting until it was daylight, without venturing to go to bed again.

July 6. I am going mad. Again all the contents of my water-bottle have been drunk during the night; or rather I have drunk it!

But is it I? Is it I? Who could it be? Who? Oh! God! Am I going mad? Who will save me?

July 10. I have just been through some surprising ordeals. Undoubtedly I must be mad! And yet!

On July 6, before going to bed, I put some wine, milk, water, bread, and strawberries on my table. Somebody drank -- I drank -- all the water and a little of the milk, but neither the wine, nor the bread, nor the strawberries were touched.

On the seventh of July I renewed the same experiment, with the same results, and on July 8 I left out the water and the milk and nothing was touched.

Lastly, on July 9 I put only water and milk on my table, taking care to wrap up the bottles in white muslin and to tie down the stoppers. Then I rubbed my lips, my beard, and my hands with pencil lead, and went to bed.

Deep slumber seized me, soon followed by a terrible awakening. I had not moved, and my sheets were not marked. I rushed to the table. The muslin round the bottles remained intact; I undid the string, trembling with fear. All the water had been drunk, and so had the milk! Ah! Great God! I must start for Paris immediately.

July 12. Paris. I must have lost my head during the last few days! I must be the plaything of my enervated imagination, unless I am really a somnambulist, or I have been brought under the power of one of those influences -- hypnotic suggestion, for example -- which are known to exist, but have hitherto been inexplicable. In any case, my mental state bordered on madness, and twenty-four hours of Paris sufficed to restore me to my equilibrium.

Yesterday after doing some business and paying some visits, which instilled fresh and invigorating mental air into me, I wound up my evening at the Théâtre Français. A drama by Alexander Dumas the Younger was being acted, and his brilliant and powerful play completed my cure. Certainly solitude is dangerous for active minds. We need men who can think and can talk, around us. When we are alone for a long time, we people space with phantoms.

I returned along the boulevards to my hotel in excellent spirits. Amid the jostling of the crowd I thought, not without irony, of my terrors and surmises of the previous week, because I believed, yes, I believed, that an invisible being lived beneath my roof. How weak our mind is; how quickly it is terrified and unbalanced as soon as we are confronted with a small, incomprehensible fact. Instead of dismissing the problem with: ``We do not understand because we cannot find the cause,'' we immediately imagine terrible mysteries and supernatural powers.

July 14. Fête of the Republic. I walked through the streets, and the crackers and flags amused me like a child. Still, it is very foolish to make merry on a set date, by Government decree. People are like a flock of sheep, now steadily patient, now in ferocious revolt. Say to it: ``Amuse yourself,'' and it amuses itself. Say to it: ``Go and fight with your neighbor,'' and it goes and fights. Say to it: ``Vote for the Emperor,'' and it votes for the Emperor; then say to it: ``Vote for the Republic,'' and it votes for the Republic.

Those who direct it are stupid, too; but instead of obeying men they obey principles, a course which can only be foolish, ineffective, and false, for the very reason that principles are ideas which are considered as certain and unchangeable, whereas in this world one is certain of nothing, since light is an illusion and noise is deception.

July 16. I saw some things yesterday that troubled me very much.

I was dining at my cousin's, Madame Sablé, whose husband is colonel of the Seventy-sixth Chasseurs at Limoges. There were two young women there, one of whom had married a medical man, Dr. Parent, who devotes himself a great deal to nervous diseases and to the extraordinary manifestations which just now experiments in hypnotism and suggestion are producing.

He related to us at some length the enormous results obtained by English scientists and the doctors of the medical school at Nancy, and the facts which he adduced appeared to me so strange, that I declared that I was altogether incredulous.

``We are,'' he declared, ``on the point of discovering one of the most important secrets of nature, I mean to say, one of its most important secrets on this earth, for assuredly there are some up in the stars, yonder, of a different kind of importance. Ever since man has thought, since he has been able to express and write down his thoughts, he has felt himself close to a mystery which is impenetrable to his coarse and imperfect senses, and he endeavors to supplement the feeble penetration of his organs by the efforts of his intellect. As long as that intellect remained in its elementary stage, this intercourse with invisible spirits assumed forms which were commonplace though terrifying. Thence sprang the popular belief in the supernatural, the legends of wandering spirits, of fairies, of gnomes, of ghosts, I might even say the conception of God, for our ideas of the Workman-Creator, from whatever religion they may have come down to us, are certainly the most mediocre, the stupidest, and the most unacceptable inventions that ever sprang from the frightened brain of any human creature. Nothing is truer than what Voltaire says: `If God made man in His own image, man has certainly paid Him back again.'

``But for rather more than a century, men seem to have had a presentiment of something new. Mesmer and some others have put us on an unexpected track, and within the last two or three years especially, we have arrived at results really surprising.''

My cousin, who is also very incredulous, smiled, and Dr. Parent said to her: ``Would you like me to try and send you to sleep, Madame?''

``Yes, certainly.''

She sat down in an easy-chair, and he began to look at her fixedly, as if to fascinate her. I suddenly felt myself somewhat discomposed; my heart beat rapidly and I had a choking feeling in my throat. I saw that Madame Sablé's eyes were growing heavy, her mouth twitched, and her bosom heaved, and at the end of ten minutes she was asleep.

``Go behind her,'' the doctor said to me; so I took a seat behind her. He put a visiting-card into her hands, and said to her: ``This is a looking-glass; what do you see in it?''

She replied: ``I see my cousin.''

``What is he doing?''

``He is twisting his mustache.''

``And now?''

``He is taking a photograph out of his pocket.''

``Whose photograph is it?''

``His own.''

That was true, for the photograph had been given me that same evening at the hotel.

``What is his attitude in this portrait?''

``He is standing up with his hat in his hand.''

She saw these things in that card, in that piece of white pasteboard, as if she had seen them in a looking-glass.

The young women were frightened, and exclaimed: ``That is quite enough! Quite, quite enough!''

But the doctor said to her authoritatively: ``You will get up at eight o'clock to-morrow morning; then you will go and call on your cousin at his hotel and ask him to lend you the five thousand francs which your husband asks of you, and which he will ask for when he sets out on his coming journey.''

Then he woke her up.

On returning to my hotel, I thought over this curious *séance* and I was assailed by doubts, not as to my cousin's absolute and undoubted good faith, for I had known her as well as if she had been my own sister ever since she was a child, but as to a possible trick on the doctor's part. Had not he, perhaps, kept a glass hidden in his hand, which he showed to the young woman in her sleep at the same time as he did the card? Professional conjurers do things which are just as singular.

However, I went to bed, and this morning, at about half past eight, I was awakened by my footman, who said to me: ``Madame Sablé has asked to see you immediately, Monsieur.'' I dressed hastily and went to her.

She sat down in some agitation, with her eyes on the floor, and without raising her veil said to me: ``My dear cousin, I am going to ask a great favor of you.''

``What is it, cousin?''

``I do not like to tell you, and yet I must. I am in absolute want of five thousand francs.''

``What, you?''

``Yes, I, or rather my husband, who has asked me to procure them for him.''

I was so stupefied that I hesitated to answer. I asked myself whether she had not really been making fun of me with Dr. Parent, if it were not merely a very well-acted farce which had been got up beforehand. On looking at her attentively, however, my doubts disappeared. She was trembling with grief, so painful was this step to her, and I was sure that her throat was full of sobs.

I knew that she was very rich and so I continued: ``What! Has not your husband five thousand francs at his disposal? Come, think. Are you sure that he commissioned you to ask me for them?''

She hesitated for a few seconds, as if she were making a great effort to search her memory, and then she replied: ``Yes -- yes, I am quite sure of it.''

``He has written to you?''

She hesitated again and reflected, and I guessed the torture of her thoughts. She did not know. She only knew that she was to borrow five thousand francs of me for her husband. So she told a lie.

``Yes, he has written to me.''

``When, pray? You did not mention it to me yesterday.''

``I received his letter this morning.''

``Can you show it to me?''

``No; no -- no -- it contained private matters, things too personal to ourselves. I burned it.''

``So your husband runs into debt?''

She hesitated again, and then murmured: ``I do not know.''

Thereupon I said bluntly: ``I have not five thousand francs at my disposal at this moment, my dear cousin.''

She uttered a cry, as if she were in pair; and said: ``Oh! oh! I beseech you, I beseech you to get them for me.''

She got excited and clasped her hands as if she were praying to me! I heard her voice change its tone; she wept and sobbed, harassed and dominated by the irresistible order that she had received.

``Oh! oh! I beg you to -- if you knew what I am suffering -- I want them to-day.''

I had pity on her: ``You shall have them by and by, I swear to you.''

``Oh! thank you! thank you! How kind you are.''

I continued: ``Do you remember what took place at your house last night?''

``Yes.''

``Do you remember that Dr. Parent sent you to sleep?''

``Yes.''

``Oh! Very well then; he ordered you to come to me this morning to borrow five thousand francs, and at this moment you are obeying that suggestion.''

She considered for a few moments, and then replied: ``But as it is my husband who wants them -- ''

For a whole hour I tried to convince her, but could not succeed, and when she had gone I went to the doctor. He was just going out, and he listened to me with a smile, and said: ``Do you believe now?''

``Yes, I cannot help it.''

``Let us go to your cousin's.''

She was already resting on a couch, overcome with fatigue. The doctor felt her pulse, looked at her for some time with one hand raised toward her eyes, which she closed by degrees under the irresistible power of this magnetic influence. When she was asleep, he said:

``Your husband does not require the five thousand francs any longer! You must, therefore, forget that you asked your cousin to lend them to you, and, if he speaks to you about it, you will not understand him."

Then he woke her up, and I took out a pocket-book and said: ``Here is what you asked me for this morning, my dear cousin." But she was so surprised, that I did not venture to persist; nevertheless, I tried to recall the circumstance to her, but she denied it vigorously, thought that I was making fun of her, and in the end, very nearly lost her temper.

There! I have just come back, and I have not been able to eat any lunch, for this experiment has altogether upset me.

July 19. Many people to whom I have told the adventure have laughed at me. I no longer know what to think. The wise man says: Perhaps?

July 21. I dined at Bougival, and then I spent the evening at a boatmen's ball. Decidedly everything depends on place and surroundings. It would be the height of folly to believe in the supernatural on the *Ile de la Grenouillière*.[1] But on the top of Mont Saint-Michel or in India, we are terribly under the influence of our surroundings. I shall return home next week.

[1] Frog-island.

July 30. I came back to my own house yesterday. Everything is going on well.

August 2. Nothing fresh; it is splendid weather, and I spend my days in watching the Seine flow past.

August 4. Quarrels among my servants. They declare that the glasses are broken in the cupboards at night. The footman accuses the cook, she accuses the needlewoman, and the latter accuses the other two. Who is the culprit? It would take a clever person to tell.

August 6. This time, I am not mad. I have seen -- I have seen -- I have seen! -- I can doubt no longer -- *I have seen it!*

I was walking at two o'clock among my rose-trees, in the full sunlight -- in the walk bordered by autumn roses which are beginning to fall. As I stopped to look at a Géant de Bataille, which had three splendid blooms, I distinctly saw the stalk of one of the roses bend close to me, as if an invisible hand had bent it, and then break, as if that hand had picked it! Then the flower raised itself, following the curve which a hand would have described in carrying it toward a mouth, and remained suspended in the transparent air, alone and motionless, a terrible red spot, three yards from my eyes. In desperation I rushed at it to take it! I found nothing; it had disappeared. Then I was seized with furious rage against myself, for it is not wholesome for a reasonable and serious man to have such hallucinations.

But was it a hallucination? I turned to look for the stalk, and I found it immediately under the bush, freshly broken, between the two other roses which remained on the branch. I returned home, then, with a much disturbed mind; for I am certain now, certain as I am of the alternation of day and night, that there exists close to me an invisible being who lives on milk and on water, who can touch objects, take them and change their places; who is, consequently, endowed with a material nature, although imperceptible to sense, and who lives as I do, under my roof --

August 7. I slept tranquilly. He drank the water out of my decanter, but did not disturb my sleep.

I ask myself whether I am mad. As I was walking just now in the sun by the riverside, doubts as to my own sanity arose in me; not vague doubts such as I have had hitherto, but precise and absolute doubts. I have seen mad people, and I have known some who were quite intelligent, lucid, even clear-sighted in every concern of life, except on one point. They could speak clearly, readily, profoundly on everything; till their thoughts were caught in the breakers of their delusions and went to pieces there, were dispersed and swamped in that furious and terrible sea of fogs and squalls which is called madness.

I certainly should think that I was mad, absolutely mad, if I were not conscious that I knew my state, if I could not fathom it and analyze it with the most complete lucidity. I should, in fact, be a reasonable man laboring under a hallucination. Some unknown disturbance must have been excited in my brain, one of those disturbances which physiologists of the present day try to note and to fix precisely, and that disturbance must have caused a profound gulf in my mind and in the order and logic of my ideas. Similar phenomena occur in dreams, and lead us through the most unlikely phantasmagoria, without causing us any surprise, because our verifying apparatus and our sense of control have gone to sleep, while our imaginative faculty wakes and works.

Was it not possible that one of the imperceptible keys of the cerebral finger-board had been paralyzed in me? Some men lose the recollection of proper names, or of verbs, or of numbers, or merely of dates, in consequence of an accident. The localization of all the avenues of thought has been accomplished nowadays; what, then, would there be surprising in the fact that my faculty of controlling the unreality of certain hallucinations should be destroyed for the time being?

I thought of all this as I walked by the side of the water. The sun was shining brightly on the river and made earth delightful, while it filled me with love for

117

life, for the swallows, whose swift agility is always delightful in my eyes, for the plants by the riverside, whose rustling is a pleasure to my ears.

By degrees, however, an inexplicable feeling of discomfort seized me. It seemed to me as if some unknown force were numbing and stopping me, were preventing me from going further and were calling me back. I felt that painful wish to return which comes on you when you have left a beloved invalid at home, and are seized by a presentiment that he is worse.

I, therefore, returned despite of myself, feeling certain that I should find some bad news awaiting me, a letter or a telegram. There was nothing, however, and I was surprised and uneasy, more so than if I had had another fantastic vision.

August 8. I spent a terrible evening, yesterday. He does not show himself any more, but I feel that He is near me, watching me, looking at me, penetrating me, dominating me, and more terrible to me when He hides himself thus than if He were to manifest his constant and invisible presence by supernatural phenomena. However, I slept.

August 9. Nothing, but I am afraid.

August 10. Nothing; but what will happen to-morrow?

August 11. Still nothing. I cannot stop at home with this fear hanging over me and these thoughts in my mind; I shall go away.

August 12. Ten o'clock at night. All day long I have been trying to get away, and have not been able. I contemplated a simple and easy act of liberty, a carriage ride to Rouen -- and I have not been able to do it. What is the reason?

August 13. When one is attacked by certain maladies, the springs of our physical being seem broken, our energies destroyed, our muscles relaxed, our bones to be as soft as our flesh, and our blood as liquid as water. I am experiencing the same in my moral being, in a strange and distressing manner. I have no longer any strength, any courage, any self-control, nor even any power to set my own will in motion. I have no power left to will anything, but some one does it for me and I obey.

August 14. I am lost! Somebody possesses my soul and governs it! Somebody orders all my acts, all my movements, all my thoughts. I am no longer master of myself, nothing except an enslaved and terrified spectator of the things which I do. I wish to go out; I cannot. He does not wish to; and so I remain, trembling and distracted in the armchair in which he keeps me sitting. I merely wish to get up and to rouse myself, so as to think that I am still master of myself: I cannot! I am riveted to my chair, and my chair adheres to the floor in such a manner that no force of mine can move us.

Then suddenly, I must, I must go to the foot of my garden to pick some strawberries and eat them -- and I go there. I pick the strawberries and I eat them! Oh! my God! my God! Is there a God? If there be one, deliver me! save me! succor me! Pardon! Pity! Mercy! Save me! Oh! what sufferings! what torture! what horror!

August 15. Certainly this is the way in which my poor cousin was possessed and swayed, when she came to borrow five thousand francs of me. She was under the power of a strange will which had entered into her, like another soul, a parasitic and ruling soul. Is the world coming to an end?

But who is he, this invisible being that rules me, this unknowable being, this rover of a supernatural race?

Invisible beings exist, then! how is it, then, that since the beginning of the world they have never manifested themselves in such a manner as they do to me? I have never read anything that resembles what goes on in my house. Oh! If I could only leave it, if I could only go away and flee, and never return, I should be saved; but I cannot.

August 16. I managed to escape to-day for two hours, like a prisoner who finds the door of his dungeon accidentally open. I suddenly felt that I was free and that He was far away, and so I gave orders to put the horses in as quickly as possible, and I drove to Rouen. Oh! how delightful to be able to say to my coachman: ``Go to Rouen!''

I made him pull up before the library, and I begged them to lend me Dr. Herrmann Herestauss's treatise on the unknown inhabitants of the ancient and modern world.

Then, as I was getting into my carriage, I intended to say: ``To the railway station!'' but instead of this I shouted -- I did not speak; but I shouted -- in such a loud voice that all the passers-by turned round: ``Home!'' and I fell back on to the cushion of my carriage, overcome by mental agony. He had found me out and regained possession of me.

August 17. Oh! What a night! what a night! And yet it seems to me that I ought to rejoice. I read until one o'clock in the morning! Herestauss, Doctor of Philosophy and Theogony, wrote the history and the manifestation of all those invisible beings which hover around man, or of whom he dreams. He describes their origin, their domains, their power; but none of them resembles the one which haunts me. One might say that man, ever since he has thought, has had a foreboding and a fear of a new being, stronger than himself, his successor in this world, and that, feeling him near, and not being able to foretell the nature of the unseen one, he has, in his terror, created the whole race of hidden beings, vague phantoms born of fear.

119

Having, therefore, read until one o'clock in the morning, I went and sat down at the open window, in order to cool my forehead and my thoughts in the calm night air. It was very pleasant and warm! How I should have enjoyed such a night formerly!

There was no moon, but the stars darted out their rays in the dark heavens. Who inhabits those worlds?

What forms, what living beings, what animals are there yonder? Do those who are thinkers in those distant worlds know more than we do? What can they do more than we? What do they see which we do not? Will not one of them, some day or other, traversing space, appear on our earth to conquer it, just as formerly the Norsemen crossed the sea in order to subjugate nations feebler than themselves?

We are so weak, so powerless, so ignorant, so small -- we who live on this particle of mud which revolves in liquid air.

I fell asleep, dreaming thus in the cool night air, and then, having slept for about three quarters of an hour, I opened my eyes without moving, awakened by an indescribably confused and strange sensation. At first I saw nothing, and then suddenly it appeared to me as if a page of the book, which had remained open on my table, turned over of its own accord. Not a breath of air had come in at my window, and I was surprised and waited. In about four minutes, I saw, I saw -- yes I saw with my own eyes -- another page lift itself up and fall down on the others, as if a finger had turned it over. My armchair was empty, appeared empty, but I knew that He was there, He, and sitting in my place, and that He was reading. With a furious bound, the bound of an enraged wild beast that wishes to disembowel its tamer, I crossed my room to seize him, to strangle him, to kill him! But before I could reach it, my chair fell over as if somebody had run away from me. My table rocked, my lamp fell and went out, and my window closed as if some thief had been surprised and had fled out into the night, shutting it behind him.

So He had run away; He had been afraid; He, afraid of me!

So to-morrow, or later -- some day or other, I should be able to hold him in my clutches and crush him against the ground! Do not dogs occasionally bite and strangle their masters?

August 18. I have been thinking the whole day long. Oh! yes, I will obey Him, follow His impulses, fulfill all His wishes, show myself humble, submissive, a coward. He is the stronger; but an hour will come.

August 19. I know, I know, I know all! I have just read the following in the ``Revue du Monde Scientifique'': ``A curious piece of news comes to us from

Rio de Janeiro. Madness, an epidemic of madness, which may be compared to that contagious madness which attacked the people of Europe in the Middle Ages, is at this moment raging in the Province of San-Paulo. The frightened inhabitants are leaving their houses, deserting their villages, abandoning their land, saying that they are pursued, possessed, governed like human cattle by invisible, though tangible beings, by a species of vampire, which feeds on their life while they are asleep, and which, besides, drinks water and milk without appearing to touch any other nourishment.

``Professor Don Pedro Henriques, accompanied by several medical savants, has gone to the Province of San-Paulo, in order to study the origin and the manifestations of this surprising madness on the spot, and to propose such measures to the Emperor as may appear to him to be most fitted to restore the mad population to reason."

Ah! Ah! I remember now that fine Brazilian three-master which passed in front of my windows as it was going up the Seine, on the eighth of last May! I thought it looked so pretty, so white and bright! That Being was on board of her, coming from there, where its race sprang from. And it saw me! It saw my house, which was also white, and He sprang from the ship on to the land. Oh! Good heavens!

Now I know, I can divine. The reign of man is over, and he has come. He whom disquieted priests exorcised, whom sorcerers evoked on dark nights, without seeing him appear, He to whom the imaginations of the transient masters of the world lent all the monstrous or graceful forms of gnomes, spirits, genii, fairies, and familiar spirits. After the coarse conceptions of primitive fear, men more enlightened gave him a truer form. Mesmer divined him, and ten years ago physicians accurately discovered the nature of his power, even before He exercised it himself. They played with that weapon of their new Lord, the sway of a mysterious will over the human soul, which had become enslaved. They called it mesmerism, hypnotism, suggestion, I know not what? I have seen them diverting themselves like rash children with this horrible power! Woe to us! Woe to man! He has come, the -- the -- what does He call himself -- the -- I fancy that he is shouting out his name to me and I do not hear him -- the -- yes -- He is shouting it out -- I am listening -- I cannot -- repeat -- it -- Horla -- I have heard -- the Horla -- it is He -- the Horla -- He has come! --

Ah I the vulture has eaten the pigeon, the wolf has eaten the lamb; the lion has devoured the sharp-horned buffalo; man has killed the lion with an arrow, with a spear, with gunpowder; but the Horla will make of man what man has made of the horse and of the ox: his chattel, his slave, and his food, by the mere power of his will. Woe to us!

But, nevertheless, sometimes the animal rebels and kills the man who has subjugated it. I should also like -- I shall be able to -- but I must know Him, touch Him, see Him! Learned men say that eyes of animals, as they differ from ours, do not distinguish as ours do. And my eye cannot distinguish this newcomer who is oppressing me.

Why? Oh! Now I remember the words of the monk at Mont Saint-Michel: ``Can we see the hundred-thousandth part of what exists? Listen; there is the wind which is the strongest force in nature; it knocks men down, blows down buildings, uproots trees, raises the sea into mountains of water, destroys cliffs, and casts great ships on to the breakers; it kills, it whistles, it sighs, it roars, -- have you ever seen it, and can you see it? It exists for all that, however!"

And I went on thinking: my eyes are so weak, so imperfect, that they do not even distinguish hard bodies, if they are as transparent as glass! If a glass without quicksilver behind it were to bar my way, I should run into it, just like a bird which has flown into a room breaks its head against the windowpanes. A thousand things, moreover, deceive a man and lead him astray. How then is it surprising that he cannot perceive a new body which is penetrated and pervaded by the light?

A new being! Why not? It was assuredly bound to come! Why should we be the last? We do not distinguish it, like all the others created before us? The reason is, that its nature is more delicate, its body finer and more finished than ours. Our makeup is so weak, so awkwardly conceived; our body is encumbered with organs that are always tired, always being strained like locks that are too complicated; it lives like a plant and like an animal nourishing itself with difficulty on air, herbs, and flesh; it is a brute machine which is a prey to maladies, to malformations, to decay; it is broken-winded, badly regulated, simple and eccentric, ingeniously yet badly made, a coarse and yet a delicate mechanism, in brief, the outline of a being which might become intelligent and great.

There are only a few -- so few -- stages of development in this world, from the oyster up to man. Why should there not be one more, when once that period is accomplished which separates the successive products one from the other?

Why not one more? Why not, also, other trees with immense, splendid flowers, perfuming whole regions? Why not other elements beside fire, air, earth, and water? There are four, only four, nursing fathers of various beings! What a pity! Why should not there be forty, four hundred, four thousand! How poor everything is, how mean and wretched -- grudgingly given, poorly invented, clumsily made! Ah! the elephant and the hippopotamus, what power! And the camel, what suppleness!

But the butterfly, you will say, a flying flower! I dream of one that should be as large as a hundred worlds, with wings whose shape, beauty, colors, and motion I cannot even express. But I see it -- it flutters from star to star, refreshing them and perfuming them with the light and harmonious breath of its flight! And the people up there gaze at it as it passes in an ecstasy of delight!

What is the matter with me? It is He, the Horla who haunts me, and who makes me think of these foolish things! He is within me, He is becoming my soul; I shall kill him!

August 20. I shall kill Him. I have seen Him! Yesterday I sat down at my table and pretended to write very assiduously. I knew quite well that He would come prowling round me, quite close to me, so close that I might perhaps be able to touch him, to seize him. And then -- then I should have the strength of desperation; I should have my hands, my knees, my chest, my forehead, my teeth to strangle him, to crush him, to bite him, to tear him to pieces. And I watched for him with all my overexcited nerves.

I had lighted my two lamps and the eight wax candles on my mantelpiece, as if, by this light I should discover Him.

My bed, my old oak bed with its columns, was opposite to me; on my right was the fireplace; on my left the door, which was carefully closed, after I had left it open for some time, in order to attract Him; behind me was a very high wardrobe with a looking-glass in it, which served me to dress by every day, and in which I was in the habit of inspecting myself from head to foot every time I passed it.

So I pretended to be writing in order to deceive Him, for He also was watching me, and suddenly I felt, I was certain, that He was reading over my shoulder, that He was there, almost touching my ear.

I got up so quickly, with my hands extended, that I almost fell. Horror! It was as bright as at midday, but I did not see myself in the glass! It was empty, clear, profound, full of light! But my figure was not reflected in it -- and I, I was opposite to it! I saw the large, clear glass from top to bottom, and I looked at it with unsteady eyes. I did not dare advance; I did not venture to make a movement; feeling certain, nevertheless, that He was there, but that He would escape me again, He whose imperceptible body had absorbed my reflection.

How frightened I was! And then suddenly I began to see myself through a mist in the depths of the looking-glass, in a mist as it were, or through a veil of water; and it seemed to me as if this water were flowing slowly from left to right, and making my figure clearer every moment. It was like the end of an eclipse. Whatever hid me did not appear to possess any clearly defined outlines, but was a sort of opaque transparency, which gradually grew clearer.

At last I was able to distinguish myself completely, as I do every day when I look at myself.

I had seen Him! And the horror of it remained with me, and makes me shudder even now.

August 21. How could I kill Him, since I could not get hold of Him? Poison? But He would see me mix it with the water; and then, would our poisons have any effect on His impalpable body? No -- no -- no doubt about the matter. Then? -- then?

August 22. I sent for a blacksmith from Rouen and ordered iron shutters of him for my room, such as some private hotels in Paris have on the ground floor, for fear of thieves, and he is going to make me a similar door as well. I have made myself out a coward, but I do not care about that!

September 10. Rouen, Hotel Continental. It is done; it is done -- but is He dead? My mind is thoroughly upset by what I have seen.

Well then, yesterday, the locksmith having put on the iron shutters and door, I left everything open until midnight, although it was getting cold.

Suddenly I felt that He was there, and joy, mad joy took possession of me. I got up softly, and I walked to the right and left for some time, so that He might not guess anything; then I took off my boots and put on my slippers carelessly; then I fastened the iron shutters and going back to the door quickly I double-locked it with a padlock, putting the key into my pocket.

Suddenly I noticed that He was moving restlessly round me, that in his turn He was frightened and was ordering me to let Him out. I nearly yielded, though I did not quite, but putting my back to the door, I half opened it, just enough to allow me to go out backward, and as I am very tall, my head touched the lintel. I was sure that He had not been able to escape, and I shut Him up quite alone, quite alone. What happiness! I had Him fast. Then I ran downstairs into the drawing-room which was under my bedroom. I took the two lamps and poured all the oil on to the carpet, the furniture, everywhere; then I set fire to it and made my escape, after having carefully double locked the door.

I went and hid myself at the bottom of the garden, in a clump of laurel bushes. How long it was! how long it was! Everything was dark, silent, motionless, not a breath of air and not a star, but heavy banks of clouds which one could not see, but which weighed, oh! so heavily on my soul.

I looked at my house and waited. How long it was! I already began to think that the fire had gone out of its own accord, or that He had extinguished it, when one of the lower windows gave way under the violence of the flames, and a long, soft, caressing sheet of red flame mounted up the white wall, and kissed it as high as the roof. The light fell on to the trees, the branches, and the leaves, and a shiver of fear pervaded them also! The birds awoke; a dog began to howl, and it seemed to me as if the day were breaking! Almost immediately two other windows flew into fragments, and I saw that the whole of the lower part of my house was nothing but a terrible furnace. But a cry, a horrible, shrill, heart-rending cry, a woman's cry, sounded through the night, and two garret windows were opened! I had forgotten the servants! I saw the terror-struck faces, and the frantic waving of their arms!

Then, overwhelmed with horror, I ran off to the village, shouting: ``Help! help! fire! fire!'' Meeting some people who were already coming on to the scene, I went back with them to see!

By this time the house was nothing but a horrible and magnificent funeral pile, a monstrous pyre which lit up the whole country, a pyre where men were burning, and where He was burning also, He, He, my prisoner, that new Being, the new Master, the Horla!

Suddenly the whole roof fell in between the walls, and a volcano of flames darted up to the sky. Through all the windows which opened on to that furnace, I saw the flames darting, and I reflected that He was there, in that kiln, dead.

Dead? Perhaps? His body? Was not his body, which was transparent, indestructible by such means as would kill ours?

If He were not dead? Perhaps time alone has power over that Invisible and Redoubtable Being. Why this transparent, unrecognizable body, this body belonging to a spirit, if it also had to fear ills, infirmities, and premature destruction?

Premature destruction? All human terror springs from that! After man the Horla. After him who can die every day, at any hour, at any moment, by any accident, He came, He who was only to die at his own proper hour and minute, because He had touched the limits of his existence!

No -- no -- there is no doubt about it -- He is not dead. Then -- then -- I suppose I must kill myself!

Made in the USA
San Bernardino, CA
27 November 2012